MINDFOGGER

Niles Spindrift is a twenty-two-year-old electronics genius, and he's invented a machine that can cloud men's minds.

It's a very effective machine. The government knows it, and wants it. They don't care anymore what they have to do to get it.

Niles Spindrift is running out of places to hide, and if he does—so do we. . . .

"Highly readable . . . intriguing!"
—*Bestsellers*

mindfogger

michael rogers

A DELL BOOK

for my family

If progress is a myth, that is to say, if faced by the work involved we can say: 'What's the good of it all?' our efforts will flag. With that the whole of evolution will come to a halt—because we are evolution.

—Pierre Teilhard de Chardin

Published by
DELL PUBLISHING CO., INC.
1 Dag Hammarskjold Plaza
New York, New York 10017
Copyright © 1973 by Michael Rogers
All rights reserved under International and Pan-American Copyright Conventions. For information contact Alfred A. Knopf, Inc., New York, New York 10022.
Dell ® TM 681510, Dell Publishing Co., Inc.
Reprinted by arrangement with
Alfred A. Knopf, Inc.

Printed in Canada

First Dell printing—February 1976

san francisco

It always begins this way: with a knock at the door. It does not matter how careful Niles Spindrift is, or where he chooses to live, or even what name he calls himself, because sooner or later there is always the knock at the door, and a smiling well-dressed man will say: "I'd like to speak to Niles Spindrift, please. It's very important." Niles himself no longer answers doors, or telephones, or special delivery letters, or even salutations on the street, but these cautions do no good at all. Even if he lived in the top of the tallest coast redwood, he has come to believe, they would most likely cut it down.

His last afternoon in San Francisco, his last afternoon with Tina, both come two weeks after his twenty-second birthday. Niles spends the afternoon at his workbench, set up in the alcove of a high bay window that overlooks a busy intersection. It is springtime in San Francisco, a brief space of sun between the grey overcast of the winter and the clinging fog of the summer, and today bright spring sunshine pours in the wide windows and across the peeling kitchen table that serves Niles as both workbench and desk.

The white enamel surface of the table is littered with small tools and electronic components, like tiny insects with silver legs. On a pile of notebooks, a soldering pencil sits in a metal stand. Excess rosin boils on the hot tip of the iron, a straight thin line of blue smoke in the still air of the room. Niles works with great concentration, blocking out both the fine weather and the roar and honking of the traffic down on the street. He slumps forward slightly as he works, his wide shoulders hunched, his dark hair falling far past his collar. Occasionally, with guilt, he thinks about his posture and sits up straight, but very quickly he is slouching again.

Next to his workbench is an unmade double-bed mattress laid out on the floor, and on the white wall above the mattress hangs a bright poster. THE ELECTROMAGNETIC SPECTRUM, the poster reads, and in five feet of colorful glossy paper it runs from long waves out to gamma rays, with inset pictures of radio antennas and prisms and splitting nuclei. Ten years ago, when Niles was twelve, and just starting off to college on the first of a series of scholarships, the newspaper photographers had posed him beneath this same poster, and snapped pictures that showed a distinctly amused little kid with slicked-down hair grinning broadly into the cameras, as if he had just told a funny story and was now enjoying the reaction of his audience. The headlines that appeared below the picture called him a genius, and indeed it would be the last time in Niles' life when he was certain that he understood everything. At least he had understood enough then to keep the poster, through college, through graduate school, through his brief career at the Labs, and by now it has stayed with him clear across the country, as little else has, to hang creased and curled and tattered in San Francisco. It is a silent and tenuous connection to a time when his life was much simpler.

His life is no longer simple, but lately it has gone well. The first phase of his work will soon be completed. He has little money, but he has managed to live in the same place for four months, a record of sorts for him, and for the last two of those months, Tina has stayed with him. Their relationship has been tight and functional: Tina keeps him from, in her words, "drowning in the clutter," while Niles gives her a place to stay during her long-term and consistently unsuccessful job-hunting. She is a Midwestern girl of great practicality and high housekeeping standards, and while Niles luxuriates in clean socks and mopped floors, he supports both of them by the occasional repair of television sets, at which he is unusually adept. The arrangement is both pleasant and advantageous, although Niles has decided that when Tina gets her job, he will ask her to move out. Theirs is a relationship with sharp boundaries and, for the last few months, Niles has wanted nothing more.

This final afternoon Tina comes in early from her job-hunting. She is a pale pretty girl just tending to plumpness in the legs and the chin, and today she is wearing a patterned dress that makes her look busy even when she is standing still. Niles closes his notebook as she comes into the bedroom.

"Hey," she says, "I've got a surprise for you." She tosses her heavy purse on the mattress and stands behind Niles to massage his neck. "I've got a nice surprise."

"Ah." Niles leans his head back. "You're learning to cook."

Tina makes a face and shakes her blond head. Her hair is shorter than Niles', and it makes her look quite young. "Nope. Better than that."

"You've got a job and you're going to support me."

She shakes her head again. "You're going to be so happy," she says, smiling brightly, "you won't know what to say."

Somehow her cheerfulness makes Niles slightly nervous. Tina's last big surprise had been a false pregnancy and an impressive doctor's bill because she would not trust the free clinics. "I'll think of something," he says. "What did you do?"

Tina produces a folded piece of paper from behind

her back. "I made us some money," she says proudly.

Niles looks at the piece of paper in her hand, bright green in the afternoon sunlight. It is a one hundred dollar bill, mint-fresh. Niles has seen a one hundred dollar bill perhaps eight times in his life and each time someone has been trying to give it to him. "Oh Jesus," he says, "where did you get that?"

Tina leans down close and whispers into Niles' ear. "A man gave it to me," she says. "Are you jealous?"

"Depends," Niles says, "on why he gave it to you."

"He gave it to me," Tina announces, "because he wants to meet you so much."

Niles closes his eyes and leans his forehead down onto the smooth surface of his workbench. The paint on the table is warm from the afternoon sun, and Tina's strong perfume has already permeated the bedroom air. "Oh shit," he says quietly into the white enamel of the tabletop. "Oh shit."

"What's the matter?" Tina asks, puzzled. "My God, we're rich, we can—"

Niles smashes his hand down on the table, and the components and tools and notebooks jump like muscles galvanically activated. "Goddamnit," he says, "didn't I tell you not to say I was here? Didn't I tell you that a lot of times? Didn't I say you never heard of me?" He stares at Tina and sees her wide eyes and open mouth and genuine surprise and his anger dissipates as quickly as it has condensed, and he turns and stares out the window. "Ah fuck it," he says. "Forget it."

"He's not a cop," Tina says softly, as if explaining to a child. "I can tell. He's a businessman." She sets the one hundred dollar bill on the desk in front of Niles, placing it gently, neatly, like an offering. "A rich businessman," she adds.

Niles does not look at her. "I said not anyone."

There is a short silence. "Okay," she says finally,

"maybe I got confused, but I tell a rich businessman who wants to give you money how to find you and you tell me that's wrong?"

"You got it," Niles says. He stares at his workbench and the sunlight glints on polished aluminum and copper and chromium surfaces. He sees his own face reflected in the side of a chassis box, hazy, as if under a few inches of water. Today, in this light, his eyes are green. Sometimes they are brown, and sometimes they are as reflectant as the eyes of a cat. At the moment he wishes he was a cat. A very big cat. If he was a leopard he would leap out the window and run up the street and disappear into the cool green shade of Golden Gate Park. It would take weeks to find him, he could be so wily. "Go give the hundred dollars back," he says softly to Tina. "Tell him that you made a mistake, tell him you made it all up, tell him something."

"I won't," Tina says, and she shakes her head. "No. I won't give it back, I need it and you need it and we could get something nice with it and I won't give it back."

Niles does not look at her. He knows that it is hopeless now anyway. "Give it back to the man and don't let anyone follow you back here. Tell him you lied."

"No," Tina says. "For chrissake, he wants to give you a job. I won't give it back. Tell me why," she says, "tell me why I have to give it back."

"You don't have to give it back."

The voice comes from behind them, from the open bedroom door, and like figures in a mechanical clock both Niles and Tina swivel to see who it is.

"I told you to stay outside," Tina says to the man in the doorway. He is short and pale and plump and balding slightly, and his face appears pressed at the sides, as if grown in a vise. He is very well dressed, his shoes shining like polished bloodstones, his tie knotted to perfection, flawless light blue cuffs circling his white wrists. He directs a smile of immense bright teeth toward Tina.

"It's yours," the short man says to her, his voice resonant in the small room, and he gives her a little wink. "I want you to have it." The man's name is Lawrence Carpenter, Niles knows, from an engraved business card he has seen twice before, once in a small house outside of Chicago and another time in a basement in Omaha. One time Niles burned the card with a propane torch. The other time he flushed it down a toilet.

"Get out," Niles says quietly. "Get out right now." He pulls a blanket off the mattress on the floor and throws it over the objects on his workbench.

Carpenter steps into the bedroom, shaking his head. "I think we better talk a little." He smiles at Tina again, smiles at the bay windows, smiles at the poster on the wall, smiles at Niles. Carpenter, Niles notices once more, always enters a room as if he is thinking of buying it.

Niles shrugs, resigns himself. The damage is already done. "You've got five minutes," he says. "Unless you get boring."

Carpenter nods and sits down on the only chair in the room. He looks at Tina once again. "Tina, honey, you would look much better without that make-up. Wait until you need it. Why don't you go wash your face while Niles and I talk?"

Tina stares at him.

"The man just gave you a hundred dollars, go wash your face," Niles says.

Tina frowns, opens her mouth to speak, changes her mind, leaves the room. Carpenter, critically, watches her go. "Not your type," he says to Niles. "You could do a lot better. You should meet my secretary."

"Keep her," Niles says, and he leans on the edge of

the blanket-draped workbench. "I'll find my own."

Carpenter sighs deeply and crosses his legs. He gazes at Niles benignly for a moment. "You're still going to be unreasonable?"

Niles shrugs. "I know what I want."

Carpenter looks around the small bedroom. "I don't think you know what you can get. You don't have to live like this. When you worked at the Labs we treated you badly. I will admit that publicly, I will put it in writing, and I will make it up to you. You could have any tool in the world if you wanted, time to work, room to work, assistants, consultants, unlimited computer time, unlimited laboratory space, a house in the woods, at the beach, in the mountains, the best damn stereo in America, you name it, and this is my promise: we'll get it for you."

"That's quite a promise," Niles says, although it is one he has heard before.

"I can back it up," Carpenter says.

Niles shakes his head. "How many times do I have to say it: just leave me alone. That's all I want from you."

Carpenter gazes steadily at Niles, unsmiling. "Dammit, Niles, I don't think you realize what's at stake here. You're acting like a child. I'm talking about your work, about the progress of your life's work."

Niles turns his back to Carpenter and stares down at the intersection. Already the traffic is building to a rush-hour snarl.

"It took us four months to find you here," Carpenter says quietly from behind Niles' back. "We can't afford to spend time like that much longer. There is a limit to our patience."

"If you want to threaten," Niles says, "then threaten."

"I don't have to make threats," Carpenter says. "The fact stands that the work you did while employed at the Labs is legally ours. The law is on our side but we don't want to have to resort to it. I am telling you this only because it's the truth."

"Crap," Niles says. "I have no obligation to give you anything."

"The courts might say differently."

"I'm certain you could arrange it."

When Niles turns back from the window he sees that money has appeared in Carpenter's hand. Carpenter is examining it with great interest, as if he has never seen such an item before. He remains silent, apparently absorbed by the little bouquet of bills half-hidden in his plump fist.

"I guess that's it," Niles says finally. "We've got nothing more to say to each other."

Carpenter nods, slowly, deliberately, and he begins to set the money down on the floor next to his chair. He smooths each bill carefully and stacks them and as he does this, he exhales deeply. "If that's how you want it. I don't know what we'll have to do to make you understand," he says. "We've tried for a long time."

"I understand perfectly," Niles says.

"You don't," Carpenter tells him. "You're making all of this very difficult." He places a white business card on top of the money. "Call me here when you want to talk. Anytime you need some help, call me and we'll talk."

"Don't hold your breath."

Carpenter laughs, shakes his head, pulls one of his pale blue cuffs to its proper position, and then he stands slowly. "We'll see," he says, "I guess we'll just have to see."

Niles calls Tina, and she comes in the door so quickly that it is apparent she has been listening from outside. She has not washed her face. She looks, a little sullenly, from Niles to Carpenter and back again.

"Show our guest the door," Niles says. "You owe him something, at least."

"Sleep on it," Carpenter says as Niles turns away. "I'll come back tomorrow."

"Suit yourself," Niles tells him. He does not move until Tina and Carpenter have left the bedroom and he has heard the front door open. Niles glances at the traffic again and then he returns to his workbench. He lifts the blanket off carefully and stands staring at the bright aluminum chassis, glinting in the late afternoon sun, with stacked circuit boards and a thick harness of multicolored wiring. It is four months of steady work, breadboarding and tearing down and breadboarding again, and now it is nearly complete. A few more weeks, perhaps only one week, and it could be finished.

Tina enters the bedroom cautiously. "I was listening to what you were saying," she tells him. "Is that guy going to get you busted?"

Niles shakes his head. "Not right away, at least." He picks up the wired chassis and turns it over in his hands, scrutinizing his workmanship. He is sensitive to the pure aesthetics of technology, the graceful turn of insulated wire, the smooth tan of phenolic board, the precision of miniature resistors and capacitors set all in a line.

"I guess you're pretty mad at me," Tina says.

Niles shakes his head. He feels cut loose and drifting and deeply, powerfully calm. All of it makes little difference now.

"I'm not mad at you," he tells Tina. "Maybe I should be, but I'm not."

"I'm glad you're not mad," Tina says. "I did it for your own good."

Niles shrugs. "Sure," he says. "Everybody does things for my own good."

Tina sees the money on the floor and picks it up. "There's five hundred dollars here," she says. She laughs and repeats herself. "Five hundred dollars. I can't believe it." She laughs again. "Like he just left you five hundred dollars."

Niles nods. In one corner of his mind he notes that it is more than they have ever left before. It is not a particularly good sign.

"I mean," Tina says, wondering at the money, "why are you worth so much?"

Niles picks up the neatly wired chassis. "This is America," he says. "Any boy can make good in America." The chassis is a device that will verify certain parts of the theoretical work he began at the Labs. Someday it will provide an accurate and simplified remote control of electrical discharge within the human brain. It promises to be a most remarkable tool.

Tina puts the money, neatly folded, into Niles' shirt pocket, and she sets the business card on his bench. "So why don't you work for him?"

"I used to work for him," Niles says. "I quit"—he shrugs—"for spiritual reasons." He begins to stack the loose papers on his desk, making sure he will remember what each contains. His handwriting and formulas are very small and tight and almost indecipherable. He has never been able to learn to write neatly. He has never really wanted to.

Tina begins to rub his shoulders. "You're so tense," she says, digging her fingers into his tight muscles. "I don't undertand. What kind of work do you do, anyway, that's so important? I never see you do any work but fix TV's."

"I'm the king of TV repair," Niles says. "They call me in when all else fails."

"Really," Tina says, annoyed, "what do you really do?"

Niles shakes his head and reaches into the big wooden tool box beneath his workbench and takes out a big claw hammer. He turns to Tina, cradling the hammer in his hands, and she steps back quickly. "I'm going to have to leave," Niles says. "I can't stay here any longer."

Tina stares at Niles, at the hammer in his hands. "What do you mean?" she asks. "Where are we going?"

Niles looks at Tina, at her pale moon face framed by thin yellow hair. "I don't know where you're going," he says. "Not with me. I'm sorry, I really am, but not with me."

Tina smiles and frowns and shakes her head and opens her mouth and closes it again.

Niles takes some of the money from his shirt pocket and presses it into Tina's hand and closes her fingers on it, and then he turns back to his workbench.

"Wait a minute," Tina says. "Wait one minute."

Niles spreads a newspaper out on the floor and sets the aluminum chassis in the center of it. He places it upside down, gently, its delicate interior facing upward like the soft belly of an animal, and he begins to destroy it with heavy blows of the hammer, smashing the etched circuit boards into fragments, powdering resistors into carbon, crushing the tiny silver cases of integrated circuits into flat useless discs. He uses the hammer, pounding steadily, until the workings of the device are nearly powder, tiny shards spread out across the newspaper and creeping onto the hardwood floor.

Tina watches this performance in total silence. "You're crazy," she says finally, "you're completely crazy, insane, irrational . . ." She runs out of words and begins to cry.

Niles sets his hammer down and stares at Tina. She is really crying and he is surprised. "Listen," he begins, but then he can think of nothing else to say. He puts his arms around Tina and she cries hard into his shoulder and holds onto him until finally he has to let himself loose. "I'm sorry," he says to Tina.

Tina sits on the unmade mattress, shaking her head, watching Niles silently as he begins to tear the pages from his notebooks and drop them, crumpled, into a wide metal wastebasket. She has stopped crying but her face is red and puffy and one short strand of hair clings to her cheek. "I don't understand you," Tina says slowly. "I've never understood you. I don't think I even know who you are."

Niles nods and continues to strip the page methodically out of his notebooks. He tries to think of something to say. "The rent is paid through the end of the month," he begins, and then Tina turns her face to the wall.

Niles rips up the separate sheets of paper on his bench and adds them to the pile in the wastebasket. He tosses in Carpenter's business card and one lighted match. The papers catch quickly and burn with a high bright flame and the paint begins to peel from the outside of the metal can. When the flames are nearly out and beginning to smoke, Niles picks up the wastebasket with a thick piece of cloth wrapped around his hand and carries it into the bathroom and douses it with water from the bathtub tap. Soggy, charred fragments of paper steam and float in the water at the bottom of the wastebasket like dead leaves on the surface of a small grey pond.

"Let me stay with you," Tina says when Niles comes back into the bedroom. Pale paper smoke hangs in the air now, covering the sweet scent of Tina's perfume. She sits up straight and speaks without hesitation. "I don't know what you're doing but I want to stay with you."

"No you don't," Niles says. "I'll make you miserable. I guarantee it." He goes to the closet and takes down his pack. What he owns will fit on his back and this is the way he likes it. "You don't want to stay with me," Niles repeats.

"I'll be good," Tina says. "We can go somewhere else. With the money, we can go back east, and I'll be good, and you can work."

Niles shakes his head, loading his books into the bottom of his pack. "It's not a good idea."

"We can live out in the country," Tina says, "and you can do your work and I can bake bread and make preserves and . . ."

"No," Niles says.

Tina pushes herself into the corner of the mattress and sits, her back to the wall. "I can't believe it," she says softly. "I really can't believe it. You're just going to walk out. You don't have any feelings at all."

Niles gathers up his tools from beneath the workbench and puts them in a thick leather pouch. The hammer is too heavy and he decides to leave it behind. He folds one notebook and a handful of partial diagrams inside a shirt and packs the rest of his clothes on top of the books and tools.

"We've been through so much," Tina says. "We've really been through a lot together."

Niles goes out to the kitchen and takes some white cheese and a few hard apples to carry in his pack. Standing in the kitchen he thinks of Tina cooking dinner, this the first time she has lived away from home, hovering as Niles sits down to eat, proud when he pronounces her first dinners delicious. In candlelight, Tina's face is beautiful. There is nothing he can do now. He takes the rest of the money, three hundred dollars, from his shirt pocket, and sets it on the table in the living room, weighting it down with a candlestick. Outside, on the street, rush hour has begun.

"We won't ever answer the door," Tina says when he is back in the bedroom. "That's what we can do. We can stay here and I promise I'll never answer the door. Never again."

Niles shakes his head and takes one last look

around. It will be easier, he knows, if he says nothing. Silence does not stick in the memory. He sees the electromagnetic spectrum poster on the wall and takes it down and folds it and slips it into the pack. Sitting at the empty workbench, he letters a sign on a sheet of graph paper: L.A. He will go see Freeman. It is the only place he can think of.

"Stay one more night," Tina says. "Let's just talk about it a little. You don't want to hitch at night."

"I don't mind," Niles says, and he stands over the mattress. "This is what will happen if I stay: the phone will ring all the time and there will be knocks at the door day and night and telegrams and special delivery letters and finally someone will come up the fire escape in the middle of the night and clean every scrap of paper and hardware out of this apartment and if we call the police they'll pay no attention. Or maybe something worse. I'm not sure anymore."

"That's crazy," Tina protests.

Niles agrees and kisses her goodbye before she knows what is happening. He is already at the door, pack thrown over one shoulder, when she says, "Wait a minute!"

"I can't," Niles says. "I can't." He looks back to where she sits on the mattress, frozen in the late afternoon sunshine, and he knows that he cannot wait even a minute. Tina will be all right. The past is a distillate of reality, a higher level of existence for people and things once loved, but nothing that one can yearn for or cling to. What is done is done. He stands in the door, and feels the pull of the work ahead. When he moves up the streambed of time he wishes to do it step by step, stone by stone, moment by moment, and never trip or fall or lose his pace.

"Later," he says to Tina, "it has to be later," and he is out the door, into the dusk, down to the freeway.

malibu • 1

There is sunlight in the bedroom. It penetrates the thin white curtains that cover the sliding glass doors at one end of the room and lights the floor, and a wall, and the foot of the bed. Beyond the glass doors Niles can see a swimming pool sparkling in the southern California morning, and for a moment he cannot think exactly where he is. In a dream, now three nights running, Tina has told him that he has no feelings, has no feelings, has no feelings, and this morning, as he faced her, speechless, he awakened into this room, nearly barren of furnishings as antiseptically white as a seashell bleached out by bright sun. And now he remembers: he is in Freeman's house.

And he is not alone.

Lila is already out of bed, in one corner of the room, barefoot, her jeans on, now reaching around her slim brown back to fasten her lime-green bra, the sides of her breasts very white. She sees that Niles is awake. "The music in this house never stops," she tells him. "It drives me crazy. It never stops." She misses fastening the bra the first time and swears. "New bra," she explains. "Listen, you know what time it is? My old man is going to be worried as hell."

Niles rubs the sleep and the last of the dream from his eyes. "C'mere," he says. "Let me do it."

Lila comes over to the bed holding the straps of the

bra behind her. She leans backward and Niles reaches up and grabs her by her smooth shoulders and pulls her down to him.

"Hey, man," Lila starts to say as she tumbles onto the mattress next to Niles.

"Hey, Niles," Niles says. "And you're Lila. It's okay if we use first names."

"Listen," Lila begins.

"No," Niles says, and he covers her mouth and frowns with great seriousness. "You listen. This is important. Do you know how beautiful you are this morning?"

Lila stares at him for a moment and then she smiles and then she is laughing and burying her tan face in the pillow. The smooth pillowcase has borders of tiny red embroidered roses, and as she turns her head Lila's long brown hair tangles and curls out across the linen like a thousand minute vines. Her bra straps hang slack from her shoulders. She is, Niles realizes in the brightness of the morning, truly beautiful.

"What's the matter with the music?" Niles asks her.

Lila shrugs. Her voice is made muffled and distant by the pillow. "I don't know. I like it to be quiet sometimes. In the mornings, especially."

"Yeah," says Niles. "Maybe so." He runs his fingers lightly up and down the perfect graceful trail of her vertebrae and Lila shudders, slightly, becomingly, and moves her head a little so that she can look at Niles with one brown eye. "Feels good," she says, "but I got to go."

Niles pulls the sheet aside and sits on her buttocks, the denim of her jeans rough on the insides of his legs, and massages her back until Lila sighs and pulls him down next to her.

Niles cannot exactly remember last night, but this morning makes him wish he could. Lila is strong and lithe and gentle and she makes small sounds in the back of her throat sometimes like the sigh of wind and sometimes the movement of water and sometimes the hard flat sound of shoveled earth. They make love for an indeterminate stretch of time, totally without referents, elevated to that kind of place where, as with the finest purest intoxicant, time is at once a second and a minute and a month.

At last the sun is high enough to cast the shadows of the eaves down onto the thin white curtains. Niles lies on his back and Lila on her side, her head pillowed on his arm, and they drift at the edge of sleep.

"Hey," Lila says finally. "I still got to go."

"Not really," Niles says, his eyes closed.

Lila begins to stir. "Where's the shower?" she asks. "You got a shower I can use?"

Niles turns and tastes her smooth shoulder, bites gently. "I guess," he says reluctantly. "Go out the door and turn left. Use the orange towel."

Lila sits up in bed and pulls on her jeans and fastens her bra.

Niles admires the smooth curve of her back. "The spine is the trunk of a tree," he pronounces solemnly, remembering an old book of yoga exercises, "with its roots in the nether regions and its blossoms in the brain. You are well rooted and finely flowered and really very nice."

Lila laughs and shakes her head. "You are so full of bullshit," she says, "I can't believe it."

"Go take a shower," Niles says. "Take one for me too."

Lila goes to the shower and Niles stretches out and meditates on the frothy expanse of acoustic ceiling over the bed. He counts up in his head: this morning it is exactly ten days since he left San Francisco, and now, for the first time since the long hitchhike down the coast, he feels halfway alive. Not ecstatic, he cautions himself, not joyful, but undeniably alive. For ten days he has sat around the pool of Freeman's little feudal kingdom, smoking dope, drinking beer, watching the automatic pool-sweeper, making great plans, trying in rare practical moments to decide what to do, and deciding each day—after considerable deliberation—that he will decide tomorrow.

And then yesterday, this girl, this dark-tanned southern California surf nymphet, her skin the color of twenty summers' distilled sunlight, clad in lime bikini and remarkable smile, appeared at the pool. And stayed on for a party last night, and in one corner of the living room did a little of Freeman's prime cocaine with Niles, and began to talk about some exotic technique of massage, and soon she was asking if maybe Niles had a room somewhere in the house where they could go and she could show him what she was talking about. And he did, and she did, and now Niles stares at the acoustic ceiling and realizes, with great satisfaction, that he has been seduced. In the mile-high cities of the future, Niles has heard, sex roles will become quite arbitrary. He can hardly wait. He feels fine.

Finished with her shower, Lila comes back in the room wearing her jeans and the fluorescent lime top of her bikini. It is only early spring, and already her flat stomach is very brown. She stands in front of the mirror and brushes her hair with intense concentration.

Niles sits up in bed, stretches, leans his head back, feels his own hair slide on his neck and back. In southern California, everything is hair and skin.

"Listen," he says to Lila. "Why did you stay with me last night?"

Lila looks at his reflection in the mirror but does not miss a stroke of her meticulous brushing. "Oh," she says easily, "because you're cute."

Niles shakes his head. He is a realist. "I'm not that cute."

Lila shrugs. "Cute enough." She brushes a few more strokes, the muscles in her back moving like smooth brown waves. "And you're crazy, too."

"Yeah?"

"Yeah. You remember what you were talking about last night?"

Niles tries to remember. Actually he recalls very little of the last ten days. It has been something of a chemical blur. "No," he says. "Not exactly."

Lila stops brushing in order to quote exactly. "You were talking about the unity of mind and body. You were talking about the physicality of intelligence." She laughs: "You said, about ten times, that I make no sense at all when viewed solely in terms of positive and negative charge."

Niles shakes his head. "Bless me," he says. "I'm such a flatterer."

"You've got incredible eyes," Lila says. "I've never seen a person with cat's eyes before."

"We're a limited production run," Niles says. "Strictly experimental."

"Cat's eyes are supposed to be the sign of a warlock," Lila says. "Did you know that? A thousand years ago those eyes might have gotten you barbecued."

Now they get me laid, Niles thinks. Times do change. "I'm glad you like them," he says. Of course, he thinks, it is a southern California girl who knows about witchcraft. Niles suspects that this mix of nice weather and runaway technology is brewing a brand of regional psychosis in several million displaced souls that will make an odd little footnote in the textbook of human evolution. In some ways he likes it. The environment may be polluted, but it is certainly not stagnant.

"Do you know Freeman?" Niles asks Lila.

"Who's Freeman?"

"This is his house."

Lila shakes her head. "A friend brought me." She finishes brushing her hair and comes over to the bed, pulling on a thin cotton top through which the lime color of her bra is barely visible. She moves with the grace of falling water. "It's almost noon," she tells Niles. "I've got to go."

Niles seems to be having difficulty letting her leave. "Hey," he says, "stay for breakfast. Please."

Lila hesitates. She frowns very slightly. "I should go," she says.

"If you've got someone waiting for you at home, you could call them."

"Well . . ." She looks doubtful.

"I'll shut the music off," Niles promises. "And I wouldn't do that for just anyone."

She pauses, looks at Niles with a half-smile. "Ah hell," she says finally. "Sure."

Freeman's kitchen is tiled and clean, bright with sun and wired for sound. Freeman, tall and blond and dressed like a college graduate student, sits behind the counter, reading the newspaper, and his girl Suzanne is at the electric range, frying bacon. Freeman is a dealer in drugs, a dealer with a rich Los Angeles clientele and good connections and guaranteed quality. He carries his wares in an alligator briefcase and rents this house, high up on a hill over Malibu where the sound of the breakers is a rhythmic pounding all night long. Niles has never been certain just how many people live in Freeman's house. There are seven bedrooms, all filled, and the people who live here contribute whatever they can toward the maintenance of the household: money or housekeeping or cooking or talent or sex or simply pleasant company. Freeman presides over all of it, pays the bills, and with a delicate touch sees to the preservation of the psychic ecology: an unobtrusive lord of the manor. Freeman had worked at the Labs doing programming, and just after Niles left he had quit too and come west to seek his fortune, which, as nearly as Niles could tell, Freeman seems to have found. Freeman is one of the few people left whom Niles will trust.

"Afternoon," Freeman says brightly when Niles and Lila walk into the kitchen. "Glad you could make it for the sunset."

"You just got up too," Niles says.

Freeman shrugs. "I was working late. Put some more bacon on," he tells Suzanne.

Niles sits Lila down at the counter and he goes out into the dark living room and shuts off the big stereo. It is programmed for twenty-four hours of music at a time and it runs perpetually, dispensing a continuous blanket of soft sound. The silence spreads through the house like some kind of slow reverberating ooze.

"Hey," Freeman says when Niles returns to the kitchen. "What did you do to the stereo?"

"I shut it off," Niles tells him. "It's an experiment."

Freeman frowns. "What about?"

"If I told you," Niles says, "then it wouldn't be an experiment anymore."

Freeman shakes his head. "Science," he says.

Niles sits on one of the kitchen stools and takes a grapefruit out of a fruit bowl and begins to cut it in half.

"You made up your mind yet?" Freeman asks him. "Or is it too early to ask?"

Niles shrugs and gives half of the grapefruit to Lila, speared on the end of a knife. "I haven't been so good at making up my mind the last few days. I don't know."

"Well," Freeman says, "the offer is still open. Stay here as long as you want, I mean it."

Niles nods. "I appreciate it."

"Take that room you're in now. Move in. Get to work."

"Maybe," Niles says. "Maybe."

"Listen, man," Freeman says, and then he asks one of his favorite questions. "Do you know what's happening?"

Niles thinks for a moment. "No," he says. "I don't."

"Let me tell you," Freeman says. "I realized this last night. Science and magic are coming full circle again." He gestures with his long arms toward some point below the level of the counter. "Like they started at the same place, way down here, a long time ago, and then they went in completely different directions. Only they started to curve back around again." His arms describe a great circle in the warm air of the kitchen. "And now we're almost back up to the top of the circle again. Science and magic are almost back together again." He shrugs. "I want a magician in my house," he says. "It's simple as that."

Niles shakes his head. Freeman is invariably a source of spectacular ideas, generally psychedelic in origin and best digested in the same state. "Try the classifieds," he says. "The heaviest spell I can manage involves fainting."

"You're worried about rent," Freeman diagnoses. "You and your work-ethic." Suzanne sets a plate in front of him and he chews on a strip of bacon. "I tell you what: for three months' room and board you can build me a TV like that one you made back at the Labs."

"You saw that set?" Niles asks him.

"Man, everybody saw that set. I wanted to sell tickets."

Niles concentrates on his food for a moment. Just before he left the Labs and did not yet know how careful he had to be, he had rewired an old television set so that it produced pictures in three dimensions. The idea itself was relatively simple and it was not entirely clear to Niles why it hadn't been done before; but the device had attracted so much attention that strangers began to wait outside his door and press him for details. Niles had finally had to dismantle the set and claim it was all done with mirrors. He tells Freeman about the mirrors. "I can't remember exactly how I did it," he lies.

Freeman taps his fingers on the counter, dismisses the idea with a wave of his hand. "Forget it," he says. "Not important."

"Here's the problem," Niles tells Freeman. "They know you know me and sooner or later they might think of looking here. It's just not a good idea, me staying in a house full of dope."

Freeman considers this briefly. "Listen," he says. "First of all, this house is nearly clean. Second, this house is never going to be busted. There are understandings with the power structure. I'm integral to the local economy. You're as safe as in church. And you can stay a whole lot higher."

Niles nods again, stares out the kitchen window. A heavy bank of grey fog is moving in across the ocean, has nearly reached the beach, will soon creep up the hillside to enshroud the house. Niles knows he could not work here; too many distractions, too much of a chance that part of his work might disappear some dark night. He has been careful for so long: the comfort would not be worth the risk. But at the moment he has no better ideas. "I'm not sure," he tells Freeman. "I've still got to think about it."

"So think," Freeman says. He hears voices out in the living room and glances at his wristwatch and finishes his breakfast quickly. "Time for business," he says, and slides off the stool. "Capitalism is such a drag," he tells Niles and Lila.

"You do all right," Niles says.

"I guess so," Freeman says. "I guess so." He goes

out into the living room and in a few moments the music starts up again from the ceiling speaker in the kitchen.

"End of experiment," Niles says to Lila as the music fills the air.

"What did we prove?"

Niles gazes up at the speaker, considers it for a moment. "Nature abhors a vacuum, I guess."

Lila leans on the counter and is briefly silent. "That was a pretty strange conversation," she says finally. "What kind of work do you do, anyway?"

"I'm writing philosophy."

"Oh?" Lila looks skeptical. "Your own or somebody else's?"

Niles shrugs. "Natural philosophy."

"Make any money off it?"

"Not a cent."

"Why does that guy think you're a magician?"

"God knows," Niles says. "I think he's trying to recast the Dark Ages. These days he may not be far off the track."

Lila toys with her fork. "Could be."

"What do you do?" Niles asks. "Can I get you a part in the Dark Ages?"

Lila laughs. "Probably not. I used to go to junior college in Orange County. Couldn't see the point of it. I made metal sculptures."

"An artist," Niles says. "Sometimes I think artists and inventors and dope dealers are the only people left who know what they're supposed to be doing."

"Don't believe it," Lila says. "All I know is that I want to get out of L.A."

Niles pauses, phrases his next question: "You've got an old man?"

"I'm living with a guy, yeah." She looks at Niles and smiles and shakes her head. "His name is Albert. I guess you could say we're drifting apart."

"I guess."

"I better go home pretty soon," she says. "Albert is going to be freaked. I never stayed out all night on him before."

"I shouldn't have reminded you," Niles says.

"I'd have to go anyway," Lila says. She looks at Niles, and there is a little edge of shyness in her eyes that he hasn't noticed before. "I'd like," she says, "to see you again, you know. However much longer you're going to be around, or whatever you're doing."

Niles puts his hand around the soft nape of her neck. Her skin is deeply tanned and very smooth and warm. He pulls her near, and they kiss, and later, when Niles thinks back and tries to pin it on a single moment, this is when he falls in love. Outside, the fog reaches the crest of the hill.

"You'll see me again," Niles says. "There's no way you won't."

Lila writes down her address and telephone number and then goes back to the bedroom to get her purse. Niles goes out into the living room to borrow a car. The living room is still dark, with soft thick carpeting and a high stone fireplace and a big heated waterbed in one corner. In another corner is a long semicircular sofa, upholstered in white leather. Freeman and Suzanne and three well-dressed freaks are sitting on the sofa, and there is the smell of dope in the air. Freeman and one of the well-dressed freaks are talking quietly. Suzanne is wearing headphones. Freeman sees Niles and looks up. "Can I borrow your car for an hour?" Niles asks him.

Freeman lifts the headphones off Suzanne. "Were you going to use my car?" She shakes her head, and Freeman hands his keys to Niles. "What's happening?"

"Got to take Lila home."

"That's too bad, man, she's really nice."

"Well," Niles says. "She might be back."

"Maybe we can have a little party tonight."

"Sure," Niles says. "Sure."

Suddenly there is a loud pounding at the door. The front door is a double slab of thick mahogany and the sound of the pounding echoes through the living room, far louder than the music. Niles goes to one of the front windows and pulls aside the heavy curtains and looks out at the big circular driveway. The fog has covered the hilltop and it is grey and damp, and along with the fog there are four police cars, two pulled up blocking the entrance and exit and the other two parked in a line broadside to the front of the house. Niles does not look for long but he counts at least eight cops, most of them standing behind the cars.

"Cops outside," Niles tells Freeman. "A lot of them."

There is more pounding at the door and Freeman stands up quickly and goes to the window and looks out. "What the fuck?" He looks again. "Call the lawyer," he says. "Somebody call the lawyer." Suddenly everyone in the living room is moving. Freeman is dialing the telephone and telling Suzanne to let them break the door down. The three visitors appear to be running in tight circles.

"Thanks for everything," Niles says and he tosses Freeman's car keys on a table and runs back down the long dim hall to his room. Lila has her purse in her hand and she smiles at him as he comes in. "Let's go," he says. "Out the back, right now."

"Huh?"

Niles lifts his pack and stuffs a book in it and ties it shut. "Freeman's getting busted." He slides the glass door open and grabs the frame of his pack with one hand and, when she hesitates, he holds Lila with the other and then they are outside. The backyard is empty and the fog is now so thick that it nearly conceals the high redwood fence at the edge of the property line.

"This way," Niles says, and he pushes Lila around the side of the swimming pool and they run for the fence. When they reach it, Niles drops his pack and locks his fingers together to make a step for Lila. She steps up and just catches the top of the fence with her fingers, her purse swinging wildly from her shoulder. Niles pushes her and the muscles in her arms tauten until she can throw her legs over the top and then she grunts softly as she drops on the other side. "It's steep," she says through the redwood slats. Niles hears a sliding glass door roll open at the back of the house and he picks up his pack, holding the frame at both ends, and heaves it over the fence to the left of where Lila has gone over. He jumps and catches the top of the fence and pulls himself up and then there is a voice from behind him: "Police. Hold it right there. That's far enough." When he hears the voice, Niles flattens out on the top of the fence and rolls over, staying very low, nearly hitting Lila with his feet as he falls onto the steeply sloping bank of ice plant.

He catches himself before he starts to slide down and Lila steadies him as he rises to his feet. The pack is twenty feet down the hillside, and past that the fog is so thick that the slope appears to drop off into grey nothingness. Niles thinks he recalls this as a deep gully that runs out to the highway. He and Lila start down the hillside, toward the pack, half-running half-sliding on the slippery footing of ice plant. When they reach the pack, they can hear the sounds of feet kicking and climbing the redwood fence behind them. "Forget the pack," Lila says.

But there are notes in the pack, so Niles has no choice. He carries it by the frame, like a suitcase, and he and Lila move up the gully, and when Niles next looks back he can see nothing except the fog.

"We'll go up here as far as we can," Niles tells Lila. He isn't sure where the gully leads but he knows they have to keep moving. When he looks back Niles can see the trail they are leaving, clear and obvious in the fragile succulent planting of the hillside. Even with the fog, they will be easy to follow.

Fifty yards up the gully it begins to narrow and they cut to the other side and start to climb out. This bank of the gully is not so steep, but the ice plant gives poor footing and Lila falls twice on the way up. Each time Niles helps her to her feet he looks back down into the fog and sees nothing.

They come over the side of the gully and stand on a new blacktop road, lined with large expensive houses. Now Niles can hear voices in the bottom of the gully but it is difficult to judge their distance. "Check the cars for keys," Niles tells Lila, and they move down the foggy road, Niles on one side, Lila on the other. The fourth car Niles comes to, a big station wagon with artificial wooden sides, has a set of keys on an American-flag key chain dangling from the ignition. Niles praises the quirk of nature that invariably leaves keys in suburban automobiles.

He calls to Lila and she runs over from the other side of the street. Niles throws his pack in the back seat and starts the big engine, and then he notices that Lila is still standing in the street. "Get in," he says out the open window.

"Hold it," she says. "You're stealing this car."

"Only borrowing," Niles says, releasing the brake. "Get in."

Lila stares at him, shaking her head almost imperceptibly.

"Get in," Niles says again. He sits, hunched over the wheel, and he speaks sharply: "Goddamnit, last time."

Lila opens her mouth, raises one hand.

Niles turns his head away. "Good luck then," he says, and he shifts into drive.

"Wait!" Lila says and she runs around the car and

slides in next to Niles. There is no one else on the road as they pull away from the curb and head down to the Coast Highway.

The fog is thick and Niles has to drive slowly, but soon they are far from Freeman's house. Niles watches the rearview mirror carefully. Lila sits, silent, staring straight ahead. As they drive south, it seems to Niles that some kind of surface tension must exist at the edge of organized society, manifested in such mysteries as keys left in suburban station wagons, and that if one is quick enough and light enough it is possible to traverse that surface without ever falling through.

"We'll be fine," he tells Lila. "No sweat."

"Sure," she says, but she does not sound sure at all. "I'm sorry I was stupid back there. I was just scared. My mind wasn't working."

"Forget it," Niles says. "You weren't stupid." When he thinks about it, he realizes that Lila would probably have been better off staying at Freeman's. Most likely she would not even have been booked. Now she is an accomplice to auto theft, courtesy of Niles Spindrift.

They pass a highway patrol car, going in the opposite direction, and Lila clasps her hands tightly in her lap and stares at the headliner of the car. "Hey," she says, "how about this? Let's get rid of this car someplace, soon maybe, and hitch to my place. What do you think?"

Niles shakes his head slowly. "I was thinking of driving to Mexico," he says. "You said you wanted to get out of L.A."

"What?" she says. "That's completely crazy, that's . . ."

"I'm kidding," Niles tells her. "Just kidding."

"Jesus," Lila says. "How can you joke?"

Niles shrugs. "I open my mouth and it comes out."

"You better let me out of this car right now," Lila tells him firmly.

"Hang on," Niles says. In another minute or so he pulls into the parking lot of a twenty-four-hour coffee shop and parks the car so that it cannot be seen from the highway. He hides the keys under the front seat. He pauses for a moment and looks at Lila. "You know," he says, "for a girl, you climb fences pretty well."

"Jesus," Lila repeats. "You are insane. Let's get out of here."

It takes them three rides and forty-five minutes to reach Lila's neighborhood in Inglewood, a smear of neon and stucco bathed in the constant roar of jet aircraft arriving and departing L.A. International. Their last ride takes them within a few blocks of Lila's apartment, and they walk the rest of the way in a smog-yellow sunset.

"How is this going to be?" Niles asks Lila. "What's Albert like?"

"Albert's all right," Lila says. "He manages a chain of hamburger places. He's into money. You can spend the night in the living room. We've got a sleeping bag."

Niles is not looking forward to this situation. He can already tell that it will be as complex as hell. He shoulders his pack a little higher. "All right," he says. "I can leave in the morning."

"I'm leaving in a few days," Lila says. "I've got a sister who lives out near the desert, past the smog. A little town named Morton. I'm going to stay with her for a while."

Niles nods absently. "Hold it a minute." He puts his hand on Lila's arm and points to the floodlit building at the corner of the block. "Is that your apartment?"

Lila stops. "Yes," she says. "Why?"

Niles points at the white government car parked in the alley just around back. It is unmarked except for license plates and an unobtrusive folding red pursuit light. "Let's think for a second," Niles says.

Lila looks at the car and her voice is puzzled. "That can't be for us."

"I'm sure it isn't," Niles says. "Humor me." He hands Lila a dime. "Go give Albert a call."

Lila nods and goes across the street to a phone booth at a gas station. Niles watches her dialing, her long hair tangled, her face very brown in the yellow light of the sunset. She talks briefly, looking over at Niles several times, and then she hangs up abruptly.

"Listen," she says to Niles when she comes back across the street, "there's something funny."

"Yeah?"

"There's two cops and a guy in a business suit sitting in the kitchen waiting to talk to me."

Niles presses his lips together, shakes his head. He is very quickly growing accustomed to surprises. "That's a lot of trouble to go to for a little drug bust." He stares at Lila. "How did they find you?"

Lila frowns, puts one hand to her mouth. "I don't know," she says. "I really don't know."

Niles puts his arm around Lila and leans against a building and tries to think. He is almost broke. He knows no one except Lila and Freeman. He suspects that he is even losing his sense of humor. None of this seems funny at all.

"The bottom of my swimsuit," Lila says suddenly. "I left it hanging in the shower at Freeman's."

Niles looks at her. "Your swimsuit?"

"I put my name and address in it. In case I ever drowned in the ocean."

Niles nods for a very long time. "That's a good idea," he says finally. "If you ever drowned."

"I'm sorry," she says. "It was really stupid."

Niles shrugs. "I don't think they'll hold you for anything. But they might ask you a lot of questions."

Lila stares vacantly at the sidewalk. "We took that car," she says.

Niles frowns, and suddenly he thinks of something. "We should have wiped off the door handles before we left it."

"Oh no," Lila says, and she pushes her hair back, tugging at the roots. "I'd go crazy in jail."

"You'll get probation," Niles says. "They might not even charge you."

Lila says nothing, hangs onto Niles' arm.

Niles looks down at her. What the hell, he figures. "You want to come with me?"

Lila holds onto him, does not look up at his face. She rocks back and forth, very gently. "Where are you going?" she asks quietly.

"I don't know," Niles says. "I've got to live somewhere for a couple of months."

"You want to go to a small town?" Lila asks, rocking steadily.

"Sure," Niles says. "A small town."

"Okay," she says, and she stops rocking. "Then come with me."

Niles and Lila spend the night in a motel in Inglewood and watch two old movies on a coin TV and make love three times. Lila charges the motel room on one of Albert's gasoline credit cards. "Albert is resilient," she explains. "I'm sure he wants me to be happy."

In the morning, sitting up in bed, she calls Albert. He tells her that an unmarked police car has spent the night in front of the apartment and does not appear ready to leave, and Albert confides that he is becoming a little worried. Whatever kind of trouble Lila has gotten herself into, he assures her, he would like to help her out.

Lila looks at Niles and speaks into the telephone. "I think I'm going to try to handle this myself," she says. "But I probably won't be able to see you for a while."

Niles, still half asleep, rolls over and watches Lila. She has pulled the sheet up under her arms, and her long hair is tangled about her shoulders.

"I know," she says to the telephone.

"I know," she says again, "this is a rotten way to do it."

"I'm sorry," she says.

"Albert," she says. "Don't."

"Albert."

"Albert, listen," she says. "It's better this way. I'll get in touch as soon as I can."

"Albert."

"Albert," she says, "I'm hanging up."

She hangs up. She sets the receiver back into its plastic cradle very gently and stares at the telephone for a moment. Then she turns to Niles and half-smiles and reaches out and tentatively runs her fingers over his hair.

"Burning the old bridges, huh?" Niles says.

Lila looks at him and shrugs. "Well," she says, and is silent.

"Sometimes you have to," Niles says.

Lila shakes her head. "Seems like I've been burning a lot of bridges recently."

"Everybody has," Niles says. "A general bridge-burning."

Lila sighs and sinks back down onto the crisp white motel pillowcase. "So what are we going to do without bridges, genius?"

"C'mere," Niles says, and she does, warm and soft and still just a little shy, and they forget about bridges completely.

Later that morning they take a bus heading east. They pay cash for the bus tickets and it leaves Niles nearly broke. Briefly, as he counts out dollar bills for the tickets, he hopes that Tina is enjoying the money he left with her. He is certain that she is. These days resiliency is becoming a general skill. Resiliency as taught in the Book of Television: if they don't renew your option, there's always another series starting somewhere. Before the bus leaves the station, Niles buys a newspaper and looks for news of Freeman's bust. There is nothing. When he calls Freeman's house, there is no answer.

The bus is a Greyhound with broken air conditioning. The town of Morton bakes in the sun at the edge of the high desert, just beyond the thick yellow waves of smog that spill out from the Los Angeles Basin, and so it is a two-hour ride with many stops and an intense heat that fills the bus like cotton stuffing. The bus is packed as well, because it will ultimately leave the state. Even near midday the freeways are crowded and slow-moving, and Niles feels like a corpuscle in the fever-struck arteries of a dying cow. He leans back in the hot sticky seat of the bus and stares at the headliner and wonders exactly what he is getting himself into. Lila, he is certain, must wonder even more.

Lila smiles at him encouragingly. "You'll like Delores," she says hopefully. "Delores is a character."

"Delores is your sister?"

Lila nods. "My older sister, who went to business school and who has always been steadily employed and a credit to the family."

"As opposed to you?"

Lila shrugs. "In high school I was head cheerleader."

"That's something," Niles says.

"When I was seventeen I was runner-up for Miss San Fernando Valley."

"I'm impressed," Niles says.

"I used to be pretty straight," Lila tells him.

"What happened? How come you're not some junior insurance executive's little pride and joy?"

Lila smiles. "I get bored," she says.

Niles nods.

"And it won't last, anyway."

Niles shrugs. "You can make anything last, if you really want to," he says.

Lila shakes her head. "I don't think so," she says. "Not anymore." She points out the window, at the endless smog-bathed grey-pink stucco suburbs they have passed since leaving Los Angeles. "None of this is going to last. No reason to get tied into it."

Niles recognizes the latest rising American preparations for apocalypse—the latest in a long series, and probably the most understandable. "In hostile environments," he says, "it's the adaptive creature that survives."

"We'll see," Lila says. "I truly expect we'll see."

Niles waits for her to go on, but she says nothing. "You bring stray young men to your sister's very often?"

"No," she says, and she shakes her head. "You're the first. Should be sort of interesting."

When the sky has become nearly blue again, the bus descends from the freeway and cruises down narrow roads surrounded on both sides by groves of big glossy citrus trees, the leaves deep green, spattered by the yellow and orange of the fruits, the long straight rows punctuated by low concrete irrigation fountains gushing clear water into the ditches.

The orange groves give way to the town. It is a small town, where the spreading fungus of Los Angeles industry has dropped only a few tentative spores. At the outskirts are packing houses and cooperatives and an ice plant, all facing onto a series of rusty railroad tracks. After the rails curve out to avoid downtown, there is a street of two-story cement buildings with elaborate sandstone cornice work and striped awnings over plate glass windows and dark-curtained apartments upstairs. One new bank with shiny aluminum pillars and smoky grey windows protrudes between two older yellow stucco storefronts. As they ride through town, a clock on the brick tower of the Episcopal church strikes twelve times. The bank thermometer reads 113°. There is little traffic and only four stoplights, hanging on wires across the intersection at the center of town.

From the bus station Niles and Lila walk about eight blocks to reach Delores' apartment, down streets of one-and two-story wooden houses, many of them divided into apartments, with wide front porches and browning lawns and sparse pepper trees that lean limply over the hot sidewalks. On some of the porches old people sit and watch Niles and Lila walk by. The sky is cloudless blue and the sun relentlessly bright. Niles, already sweating, makes some comment about the remarkable power of nuclear fusion, and Lila agrees that it is hotter than shit.

Delores lives in the upstairs of an old two-story house divided into a duplex and painted a pink the shade of a fresh sunburn on very pale skin. She is at work, but Lila picks the lock on the back door and Niles leaves his pack in the living room. They spend their last money on some beer to celebrate their arrival, and pass the afternoon in the backyard spraying each other with a garden hose.

Delores comes home at five o'clock and is not delighted to meet Niles. She seems happy enough to see Lila again, although she makes little show of sisterly affection; but she takes an immediate and undisguised dislike to Niles.

"Niles Spindrift," Lila says to Delores.

Delores stares at him. "That's a very strange name," she says. "Would you mind moving your bundle over by the door?"

"Pardon?"

"I said, would you get this thing out of the middle of my living room?" She touches his pack with her toe, gingerly, as one might nudge a recently deceased lizard.

"Oh," Niles says with a broad idiot's grin. "You mean this bundle."

Lila gives him a warning glance.

"Sure," he says, and he drags it away. If he had not already known he would never have guessed that Lila and Delores are sisters. Delores is twenty-seven, short, thick-waisted, broad-shouldered, with hair the color of

Lila's, but much curlier and cut short. As she crosses the room she moves as if she does not trust her body, as if the spirit has made only the most tenuous treaty with the flesh. Her face, where she most resembles Lila, could be pretty but for the sharp-edged expression of distrust and suspicion she maintains. She is unmarried, Lila has told him, and she works as a secretary in the front office of a storage battery factory and spends a lot of money on clothes that do not exactly fit and does some drinking at night and in the winter she teaches Sunday school for the Baptists.

It is all right with Delores if Niles and Lila want to stay for a short time. She welcomes the company. "You can have the empty bedroom," she tells Lila carefully, "and Miles can have the couch in the living room." Unless they object to that arrangement?

Niles looks at Lila. Lila shrugs: "Okay with me," she says. "His name's Niles."

That night Lila falls asleep in the living room with Niles, and Delores finds them entwined on the couch at six in the morning. She shakes Niles awake. "I thought I made the sleeping arrangements clear," she tells him.

Niles, half asleep, delivers an ambiguous grunt.

"If you can't observe the conditions of my hospitality," Delores tells him, "there is a coffee can on the kitchen table for contributions to the household."

Niles stares up at Delores. Her face looms over him like a Thanksgiving parade balloon.

Lila is quicker. "We're both broke," she says brightly.

"That's not going to do," Delores says. "That's just not going to do."

"Bless you," Niles says, "bless you," and he pulls the thin blanket over his head and goes back to sleep.

In the middle of the morning Niles begins to look for a job. It is already hot and there is still a six-pack in the refrigerator and he could quite happily spend the day reading Delores' back issues of *Reader's Digest*, but his work-ethic overpowers his natural laziness. He tires of rootlessness quickly and it seems to him that Morton could be a safe place to stay for a while. Lila wants to stay because she is happy to be out of the smog. To continue his work, and to stay with Lila, he will need money, and so, reinforced by Lila's encouragement and two cold beers in an insulated ice-cream sack, he ventures out into the midday blaze of Morton heat.

There are two television repair shops in Morton and Niles goes to these first of all. He prefers to work at electronics repair because he has a certain touch, and because it allows him to borrow a great deal of useful hardware. Television fascinates Niles the same way automobiles do, and he views himself as a loving, justly well-paid mechanic of the great American nervous system. Anything, he figures, for the sake of electronic evolution.

"Sorry," the man in the first repair shop says. "Can't help you." It is a small shop on a shady side street, set up in the garage of a house. Niles admires a brand new dual-beam oscilloscope. The man sits at his bench and solders inside the naked chassis of a big color set.

"I'm pretty quick," Niles says. "There's not much I can't fix. Give me a try."

"You got education?" the man asks.

Niles knows better than to try to explain his education. "Enough," he says.

"Sorry," the man says, shaking his head. The wall above his bench is covered with framed certificates from repair schools and institutes and seminars and special study courses. "Money's tight. Business is slow. You can't charge like you used to."

"Let me work for a few days and show you what I can do."

"Sorry," the man says. "Don't get enough work to keep myself busy."

Niles starts to say something more but the man looks into the television chassis and starts to shake his head and as Niles talks he does not look up. "Thanks anyway," Niles says finally.

In the second shop it goes worse. The owner stands behind his counter and makes a point of staring at Niles' hair. It is a larger shop and seems quite busy, but the owner says he can't use anyone else and besides Niles looks a little young and might not be able handle the work.

"Tell you what," Niles says, "I'll work for free a day or two and then you decide if you can do without me."

"Forget it," the owner says, and he starts to turn away but then turns back. "I'll pay you a quarter to sweep the floor."

Niles stares at him. "I'll pay you fifty cents to kiss my ass."

"Get out of here," the owner says, "before I call the cops."

This time Niles leaves with a very nice pair of needle-nosed pliers in his back pocket, plus a small plastic package of precision resistors and a coil of solder. It is a beginning. He is confident. One way or another, he will get his work done.

By the middle of the afternoon, Niles knows that things may not be so simple. There are no jobs in Morton. There are no jobs in southern California. No one is sure where all the money has gone, it was here just a moment ago, lots of it, everyone is sure, they'd seen it themselves. Only now it is gone. Because spending for the wars in Asia is going poorly, some say. People who have jobs to go to, keep them. People who have jobs to give, give them carefully. They want to know when Niles last had a haircut. To work in a carwash, Niles asks, he needs a haircut? A matter of taste, they tell him. When times are tight you got to watch out for your own.

Sometimes they ask if Mr. Spindrift would mind placing some fingerprints on this form? Depends, Niles would say. This form goes to Washington, they tell him. It is for the computer. Routine check, same as for all prospective employees. No, Niles says, he'd rather not. But this is routine, they assure him. Certainly— No, Niles says, and then they are very sorry but they will be unable to consider his application.

Niles comes back to Lila late in the afternoon. She has spent the day at the municipal pool and when Niles holds her, her brown skin smells of chlorine. "So how did it go?" she asks him.

He shows her his spoils—the package of resistors and the solder and the pliers. She is not visibly impressed. "Nothing else," he says.

Lila shakes her head and kisses him again. "A genius like you, you can't find a job?"

Niles shrugs. "The job market for geniuses is slow these days."

"Better luck tomorrow," Lila says.

"I got a better idea," Niles tells her. He begins to massage her neck. "How would you like to look for a job?"

"I wouldn't."

Niles tugs on her hair. "I think you're lazier than I am."

"Didn't I tell you?"

"Can you type?"

Lila shakes her head.

"Key-punch?"

"Nope."

"Fast-food?"

"Huh-uh."

"Nurse's aide?"

"No."

"Cashier?"

"No." Lila smiles. "I am totally unskilled, virtually unemployable, and proud of it."

Niles frowns and considers this for a moment. "You're good in bed," he says.

"Count your blessings," Lila says.

"I do," Niles says. "I guess tomorrow . . ." He shrugs.

"Listen," Lila interrupts him. "I think you're doing this all wrong."

"Oh yeah?"

Lila nods. "When times are tight, people get welfare. It's easy. Before I met Albert, I got food stamps for nineteen months straight. You've just got to apply. That's what California is for. Go down to the office early tomorrow, and we can go swimming later."

That night, at dinner, Delores is pleased that Niles has been job-hunting and actually smiles at him. Niles discovers that Delores is reasonably attractive when she smiles. But then he makes the mistake of mentioning his impending visit to the county welfare office. He asks Delores if she knows anyone else who has applied.

"Hell, no," she tells him. "People I know work for a living. But they'll give it to you. They'll give it to anybody. They'd give it to a chimpanzee if he could make an x." Delores snorts, and does not talk to Niles for the rest of the evening. To make up for it, Lila insists that she and Niles sleep separately that night, and Niles, in general, is not pleased by the course of events.

In the morning he is even less pleased. New sets of regulations have appeared and many questions are asked in the pale green office of the county welfare department and Niles' answers are not quite good enough.

The clerk behind the window has a flat inexpressive face and dull eyes that are magnified in the thick lenses of her glasses. Niles looks for a young or long-haired clerk when he walks in, but this bureaucratic harpy is the best he can manage. She is admirably efficient, and produces a lengthy computerized federal form.

Selective Service number? Ah, Niles says, ah yes. He can't remember exactly. Yes of course he is registered. He's lost his card somewhere, little tiny card, easy to lose. Yes he will certainly have to get another one. Social Security number? Ah, says Niles, right, he can almost remember it, it has about nine digits, only he's lost that too. Driver's license? Passport? Birth certificate? Niles shakes his head. His wallet has been stolen, he says and he frowns sternly at the harpy. Crime is terrible these days. When is the government going to do something? The clerk calls her supervisor. The supervisor is polite but very careful. It is necessary to know how the relief money is being used. Once it was more liberal, but when times are tight you have to watch things a little more closely. Budget cuts, federal directives, all understandable enough. Perhaps if Niles could come back tomorrow for a more careful investigation. Would Niles mind leaving a set of fingerprints? This might greatly expedite the handling of his case. Yes, Niles says, he is certain it will, but right now he has an appointment and his fingers are dirty anyway so perhaps he will return tomorrow.

Niles goes back to Delores'. Lila is lying on a towel in the backyard, listening to the radio. Her skin is beaded with water from the garden hose. Niles takes his shirt off and sits down next to her and tells her he has had no luck.

"No problem," she says, not opening her eyes. "I'll go down this afternoon. I've done it before."

"Maybe," Niles says, "you shouldn't."

"Huh?" Lila opens her eyes and looks at him.

"Maybe we should both keep our names off lists for a while."

Lila frowns and lies back. "Jesus," she says, "you really are paranoid, aren't you?" She shakes her head.

"Maybe not," Niles says. "Maybe I should explain a few things to you. Did you ever wonder why cops went to your apartment so quickly after the bust?"

Lila looks at Niles and shrugs. "That was a big bust. Freeman was dealing hard stuff. They just wanted to do it up right. The old clean sweep."

"Albert said it was FBI, right? Federal agents? And that unmarked car had federal plates. The FBI wouldn't have anything to do with a local dope bust."

Lila is silent for a moment and then she looks at Niles with curiosity. "They were there for you, huh?"

Niles nods. "I think so."

"Maybe that whole thing at Freeman's was for you."

"Could be."

Now Lila stares at him. "What did you do?" she asks finally.

Niles shakes his head and begins to tell Lila about his work at the Labs. He explains that two years before, straight out of college, he had been doing pure research work back east and suddenly the work had taken some odd turns and it became clear that it would be very important. Quite quickly, over the course of a month, Niles came to understand certain concepts that he did not think anyone had ever understood before. He had already designed circuitry that would provide some remarkable tools, when his work came to the attention of the Labs administrators. And that was the problem.

"That's a problem?" Lila asks. "Nail down patent rights and you'd be set for life."

"Except it's not so simple," Niles says. He names one of the largest corporations in the country. Lila recognizes the name: they are a major manufacturer of weapons. "They own the Labs," Niles tells her.

Lila absorbs this fact. "They wanted you to make bombs," she says at last.

"Not quite," Niles says. "The same principle. I refused, and they threatened to seize my work, and one night I went in and took all my notes and broiled my prototypes with a heli-arc and I disappeared. I didn't have any other choice."

"And they're still looking for you?"

Niles nods. "They seem to be looking harder and harder."

Lila's hair moves in the faint cooling breeze. "What kind of work is it?"

"The electricity of the body and the brain. How it works and how it can be controlled."

"The kind of stuff you were talking about at Freeman's that night. You can make weapons with that?"

Niles smiles. "Amazing weapons, I think."

"Then I guess you did the only thing you could. We're up to our asses in weapons already."

Niles looks at her. "You believe me?"

"Why shouldn't I?"

Niles shrugs. "It sounds strange, I know."

"Everything about you is pretty strange," Lila says. "From your eyes to the way you kiss to the junk you carry in your pack."

"You like me because I'm weird, huh?"

Lila smiles. "Sort of."

Niles reaches over and pulls Lila on top of him. He can feel her soft breasts press against his chest, and she hooks one long leg over his, and they kiss. Her hair falls like a warm curtain on both sides of his face and there is a taste of salt on her lips.

After a minute Lila raises her head. "And I'm an accomplice now, too, aren't I?"

"Well," Niles says, "maybe." He still regrets his

carelessness with the borrowed car.

"We're outlaws together."

"That's a romantic way to put it."

"Then that's how I'll put it." She is silent for a moment. "We better forget the food stamps."

"Something will turn up," Niles says.

"I can shoplift," Lila says. "I'd have to get some new clothes, but I used to do it pretty easily."

"No," Niles says, "that's not a good idea. Let me try to do it straight, first."

The next day Lila trims Niles' hair and he spends twenty minutes practicing his most winning smile in front of the mirror. The next three days he looks for a job, in Morton, and then in Santa Teresa, the larger town lower in the valley, but things do not go well. If he answers an ad in the paper, he ends up standing in a line that stretches out into the hot sunlight on the street. If he goes from store to store, he fills out interminable application forms and is told that they will get in touch with him but that maybe he should keep looking. He spends one day going through the groves, but no one wants or needs to hire an Anglo. Come back in the fall for smudging, they tell him.

It begins to look increasingly impossible. Niles has no money at all. The evenings, out on the front porch with Lila in the warm night air, sharing a bottle of cheap wine, watching the children in the street through the prolonged summer dusk, become some of the finest nights in his memory. But the days, the useless job-hunting in the harsh stunning heat, the growing sense of futility and time wasted, all begin to eat away at Niles' faith and patience. He needs to start his work again. It all culminates one night at dinner with Delores.

"If you want work you can find work," Delores tells him that night. She has had a few drinks and is on the edge of oration, gesturing with her silverware. "You have to pull your own weight in this society, that's the way it's set up. That's why things are so bad now; just not enough people willing to do their share."

"If somebody will show me my share," Niles says, "I'll be glad to do it."

"That's just the point," Delores says. "Nobody's going to show you your share. You have to go out and get it. It isn't easy."

"But if we're all sharing, why are the shares so hard to find?"

Delores shakes her curly head. "Smart talk," she says. "Twisting words around. I'll tell you who is doing a lot of sharing, and that's me." She looks at Niles and then at Lila.

"Lighten up," Lila says. "It's not for long. Then you can go back to being a goddamn hermitess, or whatever you are."

"I make a distinction," Delores says, "between family and hangers-on. I make a distinction between those who pull their own weight and . . ."

Niles, wordless, stands up and leaves the room. He takes a bottle of wine, Delores' wine, from the kitchen and goes downstairs to sit in the soft shade of the dusk. Screw Delores. He has listened to her long enough. Listening to a loudmouth is a bad way to earn room and board. The societal surface tension Niles thought he skated on has given way, and he has fallen through like a long-legged water bug touched by a bar of soap. He sits in a weathered old wooden chair, tipping back until it leans against the pink siding of the house, resting his feet up on the porch railing, drinking the cheap wine in big mouthfuls. That's another thing about Delores, he thinks. She buys lousy wine.

Lila is upstairs washing dishes, and when she finishes she comes down and sits on the porch steps. Now it is cooler outside than upstairs, and so it will remain for the rest of the night. Lila wears a thin blue blouse tied up under her breasts to expose her flat brown stomach to the cool air, and she sits on the porch steps closest to Niles' chair and they pass the wine bottle back and forth for a while, saying nothing.

"Delores is getting pretty pissed off," Lila says finally. "But that's just the way she is about money. It's nothing to worry about."

Niles shakes his head, takes a long hit from the wine bottle. "What the fuck am I supposed to do?" he says. "I'm not going to find a job here." He looks at Lila. "I've been thinking maybe I should go farther east. Arizona maybe. If I find a job and get a little money together, I could send you a bus ticket or something."

"Hold it," Lila says, and she reaches for his hand. "I mean if you want to leave, leave. But you can stay here a little longer at least. There's got to be something."

"Like what?"

"Well," she says after a moment, "like, you must be pretty good with burglar alarms."

"Yeah," Niles says hesitantly, "probably."

"Well," she says brightly, "see, there's always something."

"Great idea," Niles says. Lila is always full of criminal schemes. "Getting busted is just what I need."

"I could look for a job," Lila says. "Delores says that for half-rent we can have the other bedroom. Maybe I could just work part-time."

Niles laughs. "Don't do anything extreme just for me," he says.

"Maybe working would be good for me," Lila says. "I only hate to ruin my record."

"Well," Niles shrugs, "fuck it." He stands up and spits a mouthful of the bitter wine over the porch railing and stares at the last faint orange of the sunset. "We'll think about it in the morning. Mornings are for thinking." He goes upstairs and drags down a mattress from the spare bedroom and sets it out on the porch to enjoy the warm night. The lights on the street are dim and Arcturus and Vega and Polaris are bright in the clear desert air, and on the horizon Scorpio hangs suspended, tail curled and set to strike, and the time goes by and then it is nearly midnight and Niles and Lila are almost asleep when they hear Delores begin to clatter down the stairs.

Delores descends the stairs very loudly, like a fall of bricks. "I think she's been drinking tonight," Lila says to Niles. "I bet she feels bad about you."

Delores steps out onto the porch and looks around until she locates Niles and Lila, lying on the mattress in the faint starlight. She wears a drooping bathrobe with rhinestone buttons.

"Listen, Niles," she says, "I don't take to you too much. I want you to understand that."

Niles raises up on both elbows and looks at Delores' outline. Lila does not move. "I don't exactly understand," he says. "Tell me why."

Delores leans against the porch railing a little unsteadily. "Well," she says, and she shrugs. "Different cultures or something, I don't know, but I just want you to understand that."

Niles shakes his head. "I don't."

"Then forget it," Delores says. "But I'm going to try to give you a hand anyway. Come down to the plant with me tomorrow and I'll talk to the foreman and see what he can do." She speaks the words as if she has rehearsed them.

"Thanks," Niles says, "thank you very much." It is a great kindness and it surprises him.

"Don't get the wrong idea," Delores says. "I'm not doing this for you. I'm doing it for my sister. Somebody's got to watch out for her."

"I can watch out for myself," Lila says, without moving.

"You," Delores says. "You're twenty-one and how many different guys have you lived with?"

There is silence from the mattress.

"Seven? Eight?" Delores says. "I can't remember exactly."

"Sounds to me like she watches out for herself pretty well," Niles says.

"Oh sure," Delores says, "I'm sure you'd think so." She stares at the two of them on the mattress and shakes her head. "See you in the morning," she says, and she goes upstairs to bed.

On the porch there is a moment of silence. "Am I seven or eight?" Niles asks Lila.

"Don't pay any attention to Delores," Lila says. "She's always been that way. Only she gets worse as she gets older. She needs a steady man."

Niles nods thoughtfully. "Probably do her a world of good."

"Watch yourself," Lila says. "I think she likes you."

Lila goes upstairs and brings down a thin blanket and falls asleep on the front porch. Even with the wine, Niles knows he will not sleep until the night air cools further. He sits on the porch steps and watches the waning moon rise, large and slow and ghostlike over the groves to the east. He looks forward to beginning his work again; when he abstains from it for even a few weeks, the need builds up in him like a physical desire, a need almost as strong as that for food or sex. His work is what makes him real; an idea wired into him so deeply that he cannot hope to understand the reason, only to act out the need. As he sits on the front porch, the moonlight falls, pale and electric-blue, on the old mattress and the thin blanket and Lila's sleeping form. When Niles turns his head he can just make out the dark tan of her peaceful face and the smooth curve of her back and the slow rise and fall of her shoulders as she breathes. Some people make sculptures to celebrate the cosmos, and some people say prayers and some people write books and some people generate abstractions and all of them are suitable celebrations. It will be nice, Niles thinks, just before he sleeps, to work late at night in this fine warm air.

Niles awakens early, when the first grey light hits the front porch. A slight dew covers the porch floorboards and is cold on his bare feet. Lila awakens also, but when she hears that it is only six-thirty, she groans and carries her blanket back upstairs and goes to sleep on the over-stuffed sofa in the living room. Niles sits with Delores in the kitchen and eats toast and drinks coffee and listens to Delores' low growls as she reads the newspaper. UNEMPLOYMENT REACHES 35-YEAR HIGH, Niles reads off the front page. "This country is going to hell," Delores says finally, yawning. "That's what I get out of the newspaper. I shouldn't even read it anymore. It's all coming apart."

Niles nods noncommittally. He asks to see the sports page.

"Not a thing we can do about it, either," Delores says. "It's like being on a jet plane going the wrong direction. What can you do?"

Niles shrugs. "First thing," he says, "only read the sports page. Second thing, do whatever you can. It's always been that way."

"I've got something saved up," Delores says. "I'm ready to head for Australia when it gets too bad."

You and everybody else, Niles thinks. Pity Australia. "Save me a kangaroo," Niles says. "A cute one."

By seven the sun is already bright as they drive out to the factory in Delores' old Ford. The battery factory is a large squat structure of cement blocks, with a gold-colored stucco front and a little square of green ferns by the main entrance. It is the only building on a vast tract of flat brown land set off as an "industrial park," and it enjoys a view of a rock-strewn dry wash and a county housing project a quarter-mile distant. From the parking lot Niles looks down the valley and sees the smog already creeping in through the passes and clinging to the valley floor like a fuzzy yellow blanket.

Delores takes Niles in through the side entrance and sits him in the empty lunchroom and, quite quickly, she returns with the foreman. He is short and chubby, wearing a white shirt with open collar and pocket bulging with pens and pencils. He looks at Niles' collarbone as he talks.

"So you need some work?"

Niles nods. "I'm looking for a job."

"You got steady hands?" the foreman asks.

Niles holds his hands out. "The steadiest."

The foreman nods and considers him for a moment. "If you tie your hair back, I got a job for you."

Niles borrows a rubber band from Delores and he has a job.

Niles starts work at eight o'clock and by the first break at ten he is an expert painter of red crosses and knows that he has fallen into a very nice job. He sits on a high stool in the paint department, just past the open mouth of a big drying oven, where the spray-painted aluminum battery cases, still hot, move past him, dangling from an overhead conveyor like immense black fruit. As each battery case glides by, it is Niles' job to place a careful red cross directly beneath the positive terminal. Boyd, the head man in the paint department, has shown him the technique, can of scarlet red enamel in one hand, camel's-hair brush in the other, two deft strokes and then on to the next, no dripping or smearing or slopping allowed. Boyd is from Tennessee, red-haired and profusely freckled, and his striped overalls bulge with at least three hundred pounds of loose flesh. "We'll get along just fine," Boyd tells Niles as he demonstrates the finer points of cross painting. "Long as we make our quota and you keep up and you do neat work, we'll get along just fine." He paints a few crosses in silence. "I don't care nothing about your goddamned ponytail."

"I appreciate that," Niles says.

Boyd looks at him for a moment, one eye closed.

Two other men work in the paint department, spraying the insides of the battery cases with insulating plastic paint, and they nod at Niles but say nothing. He works steadily, his crosses blending one into the next as the battery cases swing by endlessly. The batteries move too quickly to allow him to think about anything else, so he just falls into the rhythm of the assembly line. It is extremely hot in the paint department, a dry heat that sucks the moisture from the body, and Niles eats several salt tablets from a dispenser on the wall. Several times Boyd comes and stands behind him and watches him work. "Paint's too thick," he tells Niles once. "Doing okay," he says another time.

Soon the whistle for lunch blows, and Niles follows Boyd to the lunchroom. He buys some bad food from the catering truck and thinks that Lila is going to have to start getting out of bed in time to fix him a lunch. The cellophane-wrapped sandwiches from the truck taste as if synthesized from sawdust.

The lunchroom is cool and lit with long fluorescent tubes and perhaps half-filled with people at the straight rows of folding tables. Niles sees few young faces. He goes to sit near Boyd and the other two men from paint.

Boyd stops in mid-bite of Spam sandwich and looks at Niles with curiosity. "Niles," he says, "there's just one thing I want to ask you."

"Okay," Niles says.

"I want to ask you why you got your hair so long."

Niles begins to unwrap his sandwich. "Only one reason, really," he says.

"What's that?"

"Girls," Niles says.

"The girls like it," Boyd says. "That's it?"

Niles nods. "They love it."

"Jesus Christ," Boyd says, shaking his head, as if he has suspected it all along. "These girls."

Boyd begins to tell stories of the seventeen years he worked slaughtering chickens in Tennessee. Boyd tells how he used to have to empty out his hip boots every fifteen minutes and how once, when the drain in the slaughterhouse got plugged, another worker slipped and nearly drowned. The moral intent of these stories is not clear to Niles until Boyd provides a short coda. "This factory work," Boyd tells him, "this factory work is pussy work, that's what I think. And you got the easiest job in this whole damn factory, too."

"I've seen worse," Niles admits.

"All right," Boyd says, and he smiles at Niles and shows his teeth like two rows of bruised corn kernels. "So don't fuck up."

By middle of the afternoon Niles is tired of painting red crosses and ready to fuck up. Boyd's warning was remarkably astute. Niles cannot take part in any large-scale man-made system without very quickly developing a deep desire to subvert it. When he was a child, it had been simple systems; a few blocks of telephones, perhaps, or a square mile of television receivers. In San Francisco, in idle moments, he had evolved an ingenious project, unconsummated, that involved a mile and a half of traffic signals plus the local civil defense network. Already, in the factory, he is be-

ginning to wish he could do something other than crosses. The Christian motif is catchy, he thinks, but it wears
quickly.

With an effort, he puts the idea out of his head. He
is not going to fuck up. He needs this job, for food and
for rent and for work and for Lila. He will not fuck up.

About three, Boyd speeds the conveyor up slightly
and Niles has to concentrate to keep his work neat.
"Must be selling a lot of batteries," Niles says, as the
endless aluminum cases parade past him.

"You bet," Boyd says. "That's how come you got
this job. Business never been better."

"Harder than hell to find jobs these days," Niles
says.

"You come to the right place," Boyd tells him.

Just before quitting time the foreman comes by and
pulls Niles off the line and takes him around to see the
rest of the plant. The foreman is as proud of the factory as if it were his own home, and he gives Niles a
detailed tour.

Next to the paint department is the loading dock,
piled high with thick silver-grey bars of lead ready to
be melted into plates, and wooden pallets covered with
empty battery cases and the empty plastic bottles that
are filled with prepared electrolyte. "Won't be long
now," the foreman says, "and we'll be set up for plastic
molding and aluminum casting, too. The whole process
right in this plant. Got to do it to meet demand."

They walk by the squat black casting furnace that
turns out immense stacks of perforated lead battery
plates, thin lacy sheets of lead. The air around this furnace is so hot and dry that sweat evaporates as quickly
as it appears and leaves a salt skin on the forehead.

"Electrolyte department," the foreman says and he
hands Niles a pair of safety goggles. Beyond the lead
furnace are wide concrete vats filled with acid, slowly

stirred by long mechanical paddles, tended by men covered with protective aprons and elbow-length gloves. On the walls are emergency showers with chain pulls, and round white porcelain eyewashes that start with the stamp of a foot. "Seven months accident-free," the foreman says, "and coming up on the record."

In the center of the plant the battery cases travel on a series of belt conveyors, past the assembly women, who do light soldering and use electric bolt drivers to secure the bundles of plates into the plastic cells. There are a few girls on the assembly line who are cute and whom Niles had not noticed in the lunchroom. They look to be young and their workclothes are new, and in the factory they appear strikingly collegiate. He stares too long, and when the foreman sees the direction of his gaze he nudges Niles in the ribs. "Don't touch," he says, smiling. "Management's kids. Summer jobs."

The plastic cells are sealed and placed in the aluminum cases that Niles marks for polarity. Dry-charged, the batteries are packed with bottles of electrolyte in heavy square cardboard boxes and finally taken out back to the shipping dock, stacked ten high on the wooden pallets, waiting for the truckers in the cool shade beneath a sheet aluminum roof. "Two thousand a day," the foreman says. "Up from two hundred just five years ago. You're getting in near the start," he tells Niles. "This could be a very big factory some day."

"I'm glad for the job," Niles says.

"Well," the foreman shrugs, "Delores told me about you saving up to buy that ring for her kid sister. I figured you could use a hand."

"Ring," Niles says, "right," and then the five o'clock whistle blows and the foreman takes Niles up to the front office, which is silently air-conditioned, with carpeted hallways and dark wood paneling and brushed metal trim, and leaves him with Delores. Delores works in a small cubicle that contains two other desks, both already empty.

"Just a second," Delores says, and Niles sits down and unbends paper clips while she finishes typing a letter on a big charcoal-grey electric typewriter. The type hits the paper like tiny puffs of compressed air. "All right," she says, when she is done, "how was it?"

"Fine," says Niles, "it's a good job. What kind of ring am I buying for Lila?"

"I think you've already got one through her nose," Delores says. "I had to make up a little story. I promised the foreman you'd invite him to the wedding."

"He has to bring his own dope," Niles says.

Delores shakes her head. She has forms for Niles to fill out, about references and next-of-kin and previous employment and general life-data.

"Do these go to the government?" Niles asks her.

Delores says no. Niles is very good at fabricating forms, and these give him no difficulty until he comes to one with blank spaces for fingerprints. "Hey," he says, "can we skip these fingerprints?"

Delores looks at him. "No," she says, "we can't."

Niles pauses, taps his fingers on the desktop.

"You got something to hide?" Delores asks.

Niles shrugs. "I don't believe in them," he says. "Infringement of my—"

"Okay," Delores interrupts him. "You have to go down to the sheriff's office to get those done anyway. They're closed by now. I'll file these, and you'll have to do it later." She looks at Niles closely for a moment. "If I forget," she says, "you be sure to remind me."

"Of course," Niles says, and he finishes the rest of the forms with a burst of speed and hands the pile to Delores. She glances over them briefly. "I thought your eyes were brown," she says, looking up.

Niles moves his head slightly from side to side. "Function of the angle."

"That's amazing," Delores says. "You have amazing eyes."

"Lila says it means I'm a warlock."

Delores nods, still watching his eyes. "I figured you must be good for something." She looks back down at the forms.

"Listen," Niles says, "why don't you tell me why you don't like me?"

"What?"

"What do you have against me?"

Delores frowns. "I don't have anything against you."

"That's not what you said last night."

"Well . . ." Delores picks up her pen.

"I want to know," Niles says. "Tell me."

Delores stares at her typewriter. "I don't know," she says. "It's morality, I guess. We have different moral systems. Your generation is different than mine."

"My generation," Niles says, "is almost your generation. I don't see the difference."

"It's the morals," Delores says. "The morals changed. I don't know why. Maybe it depends on whether you were born before or after television. But we began as animals and I think we're going to end up that way."

"I think we're just getting away from being animals."

Delores shakes her head and returns to shuffling the forms. "Dull your mind with chemicals, run in packs, mate with everybody you meet, tell me that's not being an animal."

"Who does that?" Niles asks. "How can I join?"

"See?" Delores says. "You can't even be serious about anything."

"I can be serious if it deserves it."

"All right," Delores says. "You don't think it's serious. I do. We have different standards."

"I guess so," Niles says.

"I don't think we need to talk about it anymore," Delores says, and she stands up and begins to file Niles' forms. "My sister is old enough to decide how she wants to live."

"There we agree," Niles says.

"I'm glad," Delores says, without enthusiasm. "Let's go home."

Delores leads him out the front entrance, and Niles notices that the closer one moves to the front of the building the finer and more lush the furnishings become. They walk into the reception room, where the carpeting is even thicker and the air even cooler and the chairs real leather. The factory must be doing well indeed, Niles thinks.

In a lighted glass showcase against one wall are samples of the different sizes of battery the factory produces, set on glass shelves, gleaming like jewelry under the showcase lights. Niles looks more closely and decides that the batteries have been waxed and polished. "Let's go," says Delores.

"Wait a minute," Niles says, because he sees something he does not understand.

"What?" Delores is already at the swinging glass door, and she looks back impatiently.

Niles points to the framed color photographs on the wall opposite the glass display case. They are big eight-by-ten glossy color prints, of camouflage-painted tanks and armored personnel carriers and amphibious assault vehicles and two olive-drab helicopters over a fire-spotted jungle and a riot-control truck covered with barbed wire and equipped with a hood-mounted machine gun. "Hey," he says softly, although he already knows the answer. "What are these?"

Delores pauses at the door and glances back at the

pictures. "Our customers," she says. "Our satisfied customers."

"Jesus," Niles shakes his head and he stares at the
pictures. He should have guessed. He should have
asked. "I didn't know . . ."

"Sure," Delores says. "What did you think? This is
important work. We're not just making any old kind of
battery."

"No," says Niles, very slowly, and he looks at the
bright color prints for a long time. The guns and the
mud and the flames are surrounded by thick frames of
oiled walnut. "No," he says finally, when he turns
away, and then he smiles at Delores in the doorway. "I
guess we're not."

It is a warm Saturday afternoon and Lila has said nothing for a long time. She and Niles have just finished carrying an old metal workbench upstairs.

"Don't do it," Lila says at last, as she sits on the bed, her face unsmiling above the white expanse of her T shirt. "I mean it," she says seriously. "What you're thinking of is insane."

Niles, at the other side of the bedroom, runs his hand over the smooth masonite top of the bench, purchased this morning at a used furniture store for ten dollars of his first paycheck. It is the nicest workbench he has had for a long time—since leaving the Labs, he thinks—and at the moment he considers it the crowning touch to the newly furnished bedroom. In another few days he will begin his work again.

"You're not even listening to me," Lila says, "goddamnit, *listen* to me."

Niles already knows what Lila is going to say because she has been saying it all day. "I'm listening," he tells her. "I am." He goes over to the narrow closet and removes his pack and leans it against the sturdy metal side of the bench.

"You've worked there one week," Lila says reasonably, "just one week, and already you want to wreck things. Didn't we decide we'd be careful? I thought everything was all set for a while."

"I explained to you," Niles says. "I have to do it. I couldn't work in the factory without doing this."

"No," Lila says, "forget that shit, I mean it. Listen," she says, "why do we have to stay here at all? Work another week, make some money, and then let's leave."

Niles already starts to shake his head; he has heard this all before.

"We can go up north," she says. "I've already told you, I know this guy with land. He might let us move in. It's nearly in Oregon, no factories, no smog. He's got horses and cows and a big garden, and nobody would ever find you there."

Niles is silent. He does not look at Lila. "I can't," he says finally, "you know that."

"You can," Lila says. "You just have to *do* it."

Niles shakes his head again. "Horses," he says, "and cows and a big garden and no smog and no factories, and no electricity either."

Lila raises her hands, palms up, lets them drop.

"I can't," Niles says. "I need electricity, I need hardware, I need people. Maybe in two months, when the work is done. But not now."

"Two months," Lila echoes him. "In two months the only kind of farm you're going to be on, they keep you in leg chains."

"I know what I'm doing." Niles says. "You worry too much."

"You don't worry enough, genius."

Niles shakes his head. "I worried last week," he says. "This week, no worrying." He reaches into his pack and finds the leather pouch of tools and sets it out on the workbench, and then burrows beneath books and clothes to the bottom of the pack and removes the tattered remains of the electromagnetic spectrum poster. He hangs the poster over the workbench and then steps back to admire the effect. At last Niles knows he is home again. Home is where the heart is, he thinks, but also the tools.

He goes over and sits on the bed next to Lila. He circles her bare ankle with his hand, but she makes no move to respond. She sits, beautiful and still sullen, and Niles realizes it was a serious mistake to tell her the idea that has formed in his mind as inevitably as rain in a cloud.

"You're like a little kid," Lila says. "You see something crazy to do and you won't listen to sense."

"It will be undetectable," Niles says patiently. "All I want to do is stop the factory and I know how to do it and never get caught. I'm not going to hurt anyone, I'm not going to damage anything, I'm just going to stop that factory." He shrugs. "Maybe it won't even work." Niles squeezes the back of her neck softly. "It's going to be fine. Nothing to worry about."

Lila shakes her head, and looks away from Niles. "You're going to wreck things," she says. She says it calmly, carefully, recitatively, as if she has known it all along and is now only articulating it for the first time. "Why should I stay around to watch you wreck things?"

"No," Niles says, "I'm—"

"Listen," Lila interrupts him. She turns and stares at him. "Listen: you're the one who told me you can make things last. So why can't things be a little bit stable for a while? Why do things have to keep changing around? Why do things come together and break up so goddamn fast you don't have time to think about them anymore? Why doesn't anything last, not even for a little while?"

"Hey," Niles says, "hey, we're going to last for a while." He puts his arms around Lila and she presses her face into his shoulder and Niles can feel her shaking her head, no, no, no. "Yes," he says, afraid she will cry, not knowing what to say. "Believe it."

Lila leans back and looks at him, no sign of tears in her eyes. "All right," she says, "I'll believe that you're going to get busted so fast it will make your head spin. You know what kind of time you'll do for screwing with a defense plant?"

"I'm not doing any time," Niles says, "for anything. I'm going to handle this so smooth—"

"You're a fool," Lila tells him. "You're smart, but sometimes you're a fool. There's so many things you don't see. You act like you're ten years old."

"I know what I have to do," Niles says.

"That's bullshit. You think you're a superhero in some idiot comic book."

"There's nothing to argue," Niles says. In his mind, the factory has come to represent all the things that make his kind of life impossible. "It's something I have to do."

"So do it," Lila says. "I don't give a goddamn." She gets off the bed in a single smooth movement and goes over to the dresser and begins to brush her hair, back to Niles.

"All right," Niles says, feeling a sudden raw anger. He wanted her to understand, maybe even to applaud a little, and so now he speaks without thinking. "Maybe they need a milkmaid up at that farm," he says. "I guess there's nothing to make you stay here."

Lila says nothing. Niles walks to his workbench and opens the big metal drawers and puts his tools away, as the most conscious of silences fills the room. The tools do not occupy even one drawer, but Niles knows he has enough to do the job. It will be an easy job and good experience and the most important of his experiments. He makes himself think about the experiment, and begins, with exaggerated concentration, to tin the tip of his soldering iron.

"Okay," Lila says. She is looking at the reflection of

Niles' back in the mirror over the dresser. "Okay," she says, and now her voice is much softer. "I give a god-damn. But what you're doing is still stupid."

Niles is not going to give in so easily. "I don't know," he says, without turning, examining the tip of the soldering iron. "If it's stupid, then why should you stay around? You're supposed to be a survivor-type."

"I can believe in you and still think you're doing something stupid," Lila says. "I'm sorry, but that's the way it is."

"Well," Niles says.

"Come off it," Lila says.

Niles shrugs and turns around. "What would life be without a little stupidity?" He walks across the room and Lila comes into his arms.

"I'll even wait for you when you get busted," Lila says into his ear, "as long as you don't get more than one-to-ten. There's some nice land north of San Quen-tin."

"Okay," says Niles, smiling over her shoulder into the dresser mirror, "it's a deal."

The rest of the afternoon Niles and Lila spend fixing up their room. Niles has given half his paycheck to De-lores for food and rent and saved part of it for the workbench and some hardware, and with the rest he and Lila buy a few furnishings for the room. They have made a good deal at the bargain store and left with a real bed with box springs and a metal frame and a wooden headboard—not just a mattress on the floor this time, but a real bed. Because neither of them owns much, the room persists in looking bare. They wash windows and walls and hang a few prints and Niles puts up a light bulb inside a paper lantern and Lila cuts up printed bedspreads and hems them into curtains for the two windows. It will take them a few weeks to ac-cumulate a comfortable density of disposable junk, but

even so, with the paycheck and the new furnishings, today seems like an official moving-in, and they are both
satisfied, and the late afternoon sun slanting liquid
through the clean windows and the new curtains fills
the room with a warm diffuse energy. In lives that are
filled with comings and goings, the goings become rit-
ual and then automatic, but the arrivals remain very
important. Even if they remain only a month, the room
has become a place. "Hey," Lila says at last, with some
wonderment, "it looks like someone lives here."

"Damn right," Niles says. "We do."

For dinner, to celebrate, they eat steaks and have a
bottle of wine. Partway through dinner Delores confides that in fact she is sort of glad to have people
around the house again and she's glad that it is Niles
and Lila and she's just in general glad, and then there
is a silence which Niles fills by offering a toast to the
future.

"To the future," Delores repeats.

"To the future," Lila says, and they drink, and then
under her breath Lila adds: "Unless somebody fucks it
up."

Niles ignores her and she smiles at him and Delores
goes out into the kitchen to break out the twelve-dollar
Scotch, so they can toast the goddamn future right.

The future begins well. Events and people have slid together with the interlocking precision that makes Niles
feel he must be doing something right, and the next
two weeks glide by with a regular suspended grace like
battery cases on the overhead conveyor.

Each day in Morton, the heat seems to increase, and
soon heat waves shimmer above the pavement even before the downtown chimes strike nine. The attic above
Delores' apartment traps both the rising heat from the
duplex and the direct radiation of the sun, and by the
time Niles and Delores come home from the factory at

five, the ceiling is too hot to touch. One day Lila has
Niles stand on the kitchen table to feel the ceiling and
verify this odd fact for himself so he will understand
why she spends so much time at the municipal pool.
She tries to start a small garden in the backyard, but
the soil is so packed and the sun so intense that it is
not very successful. Lila also begins to use Niles' bench
during the day to make small metal sculptures, with a
propane torch and brass or steel brazing rod. "You're
my first patron," Lila tells Niles. "When I'm rich and
famous you can write a book about me."

"When you're rich and famous," Niles says, "I'll
come to visit and you'll have your butler throw me
out."

Because Delores works in the air conditioning of the
front office, the heat of the apartment at the end of the
day leaves her limp and barely able even to remove her
chilled glass from the refrigerator. Lila, to be helpful,
learns to mix a variety of cooling cocktails with
chipped ice and fruit juices.

Niles spends his day making red crosses at the
mouth of the paint-drying furnace and is quickly accustomed to any kind of heat. Over the course of the
weeks he watches his body learn to reject heat with
maximum efficiency. One day, when the conveyor has
temporarily stopped, he spends fifteen minutes staring
at the inside of his forearm and comes to conclude, as
gusts of heat issue from the furnace, that his sweat
glands have developed a remarkable kind of transient
response. "What the fuck you looking at?" Boyd asks
him.

"My sweat," Niles tells him.

"You don't know nothing about sweat," Boyd says
"Keep looking."

Several moments of intense pleasure regularly punc-
tuate Niles' day. The first occurs on the front porch,
just past five o'clock, when Niles takes off his sweat-

soaked workshirt and leans back in the shade and opens a cold condensate-covered can of beer freshly carried from the refrigerator, and pours the chill liquid down his dry throat. It is a moment he anticipates all day.

A second moment takes place after dinner, when Niles sits at his bench to work, while Delores watches television in the living room and Lila wanders between bedroom and living room reading or sewing or using emery cloth to polish the solder joints of her sculptures. Sometimes she stands behind Niles and watches him. There is a tacit agreement between them that they will not argue about how the device will be used, so her appreciation is purely aesthetic. "What does this do?" she will ask Niles occasionally, pointing to one of the tiny components that are beginning to cover the vectorboard, and Niles will give her some answer in terms of electrons or charges or holes.

She shakes her head. "Makes no sense," she says. "What do they *look* like?"

"Anything you want them to," Niles tells her. "A basketball or a package of waves or a Sears Roebuck catalog. They're all just models, anyway."

"Magic," Lila says. "Rationalized magic."

"No," says Niles. "The opposite of magic. Anti-magic. Everything here has a handle on it. That's what makes it possible."

"Maybe," Lila says, but her southern California sense of technologic wonder is clearly unsatisfied. "But maybe not."

The third fine moment of the day happens when Niles has finished with his work, has put his tools away, has sat out on the front porch for a few minutes to watch the stars, and at last is ready for bed. Lila has begun to get up with Niles and Delores in the morning, so she goes to bed early and is usually almost asleep when Niles slides in beside her. It is hot at night and they sleep with only a sheet and Lila is always framed in the whiteness of the bed linen with the natural curved grace of a badger or marmot against a snowbank. She moves drowsily, smells sweet, feels soft, holds tight. Before he sleeps, Niles often thinks that sometimes we live at the pace of may flies and everything happens too fast, and sometimes at the pace of trees, and nothing happens at all. Sometimes we are leaves caught in a stagnating pool and sometimes we fall into rapids, but once in a while we hit on our own pace in time, exactly, and then there is no better feeling. These moments mark the progression of Niles' days in Morton like the deliberate beats of a long slow clock.

Quite quickly, Lila resigns herself to spending a few months in Morton while Niles finishes his work. Even so, she extracts a promise from him that before the end of the summer, they will spend some time in the mountains. "Someday," she tells Niles, "the mountains might be the last place we have to go."

Hardly a day passes in Morton that she does not produce some bit of evidence for the apocalypse. One evening, while Niles is at his workbench, she comes into the bedroom holding a can of spray deodorant.

"Did you read the label on this thing?" Lila asks him.

Niles glances up absent-mindedly. "I don't think so," he says.

"There's a chemical in this can," she says, "that produces brain lesions in human beings."

"It says that on the can?"

Lila shakes her head. "I read it in the paper."

Niles stares at the can briefly. "I never use it, anyway," he says.

"You know what this means to me?" Lila asks him. "This says that we're burning out our brains to make our armpits smell sweet."

"Confused priorities," Niles says.

"Damn right," Lila agrees, "and getting more confused every day."

By now Niles knows just where this leads. He turns back to his workbench, the smoking soldering iron, a tiny integrated circuit held captive in a heat sink. "I promise," he says, "before the end of the summer, we'll go to the mountains."

"It's important," Lila says, "I swear to god, it's important."

At this point, however, nothing is so important to Niles as his work. One weekend he and Lila drive Delores' car into Los Angeles and he buys most of the parts that he will need, and his second paycheck evaporates as quickly as a bead of sweat in the Morton heat. He is duplicating the device he nearly completed in San Francisco, and having done it once he sees shortcuts and simplifications that were not apparent in the first model. He miniaturizes it as well, using more pieces of integrated circuitry, so that it will be easier to conceal in the factory. Since it will run nearly heatless, the packaging can be very dense, and Niles manages the best workmanship he has yet done—no space wasted, yet everything laid out with symmetry and logic and precise economy. The device has grown to be a highly evolved bit of hardware.

Soon he is working four or five hours a night. Lila puts up with it because Niles assures her it will only be for a short time longer; the sooner he finishes, he tells her, the sooner they can go to the mountains. Delores is initially very curious about what Niles is doing and he devises some long story about practicing for a certain kind of license that will allow him to work as a television repairman. Delores approves this wholeheartedly: she likes to see a young man improve himself, and she would also like to have her television repaired for free. Niles has already fixed a small radio for her and she swears that he has a real touch.

His theoretical work—the pages of notes and equations that fill his notebooks—has reached a standstill. He has encountered obstacles in his theory that will remain until his practical experiment is completed. If it works as Niles expects it to, it will validate the basis of his expectations and open a series of possibilities that stretch out into the future as endlessly as reflections in a pair of opposed mirrors. He even dreams this image at night: himself, alone in a strangely featureless barbershop, strapped into a chair, staring into mirrors that toss his repetitive and diminishing reflection back and forth across the room and infinitely, immutably, into the greenish haze of the mirror's territory.

On a Wednesday night late in June, far ahead of his schedule, the device is completed, and Niles tests each subcircuit and determines that when he applies power, at least nothing will cook. He wires two acid-filled nickel-cadmium batteries, purchased war-surplus, into place, checks their connections, and sets the small metal chassis in the center of his bench. He expects it will have an effective range of several hundred square yards, and for this first test he turns down the gain and hopes it will extend no farther than the perimeter of the bedroom. In the living room Niles can hear the television and the sound of Delores' laughter, the canned and real mirth blending like contrasting pigments. In the kitchen Lila is making noise with a set of pans. He runs one finger tentatively across the smooth side of the chassis and then, without hesitation, he thumbs the tiny microswitch set into the top of the case. It is operating.

Niles sits back in his chair. It certainly is a comfortable chair. He feels as if he could sit in this comfortable chair forever and ever, except he knows he can't.

He can't because he has so much to do. He is very busy. He can't quite remember what it is he is supposed to be doing, but he knows he is very busy. He sees the little aluminum box on his workbench and suddenly remembers that this is what he is supposed to be doing. He built the aluminum box. He stares at the box for a long time and finally, with a great effort, he thinks: it works. It works, he thinks, yes it does. And then he is puzzled again: the thought has slipped his mind. What works? He sits, enjoying the comfortable chair, drifting along, and finally remembers the box again, and then he thinks he should call Lila to come and see it. Yes he certainly should call her, he thinks, and some time passes, and he is still thinking that he should call her to come in and see the box but somehow he just doesn't seem to be getting around to it, and so he sits for a while longer looking at nothing in particular and thinking that he really should call what's-her-name but that there is no real hurry.

Finally Lila comes in to see why Niles has been so quiet. She has been baking in the kitchen and she walks in the door with a bowl of half-kneaded bread dough in her hands and as soon as she is in the room she sits down on the bed and smiles. She sets the bowl of dough on the floor and smiles at Niles and he smiles back at her but they say nothing. They smile for a long time and Niles thinks how relaxed and beautiful Lila looks and how he could sit in this comfortable chair and watch Lila for the rest of the night. Except that there is something he should try to remember. There is something very important that he is supposed to remember and it has nothing to do with how beautiful Lila looks and it is so important that he should try very hard to recollect.

It is taking him a long time to go through the steps and he feels as if each thought is a mountain to be climbed. Lila is in the room. He has wanted Lila to come in. He had wanted her to come in so that he could show her something. He had wanted her to come in the room so that he could show her the . . . Niles closes his eyes and thinks very hard and opens them and sees the box. The box. The microswitch is bright red plastic and it stands out on the aluminum chassis like a beacon. He should touch that switch, Niles thinks—more than anything else, that is important and he should do it—and he reaches out and touches the switch and the box goes dead.

Lila is still sitting on the bed and she is still smiling, except now it is the artificial smile of one posing for important photographs. The smile fades quickly and then she is blinking her eyes, as if she has just come into a brightly lit room. Niles picks up the little aluminum chassis and holds it in his hand. His head is still empty but already his body is flushing with the adrenalin exhilaration of sudden and long-sought success. "It works," Niles says softly, to himself, "it works, it works, it works."

By now Lila's smile has faded into bewilderment. Her eyes wide, she looks from floor to ceiling, corner to corner of the room as if searching for bats or mice. "What the hell was that?" she asks slowly. "What just happened?"

Niles tries to explain that it is completely harmless and temporary. "Minute alterations in neural resistivity," he begins, but Lila only stares at him, her face pale, and she says she needs some fresh air.

Niles takes one of her arms and leads her down to the front porch. The night air is cool and the sky clear and starry but Lila does not notice. They sit on the porch steps and she shakes her head gently, like a swimmer dislodging persistent water from a plugged ear. "That's crazy," she says finally. "That's very very strange."

"It's all right," Niles says. "That's exactly what it's supposed to do."

Lila looks at him for a moment. "And you think you're going to put that in the factory?"

Niles nods.

She shakes her head again. "Don't," she says. "Keep it to yourself. Hide it. Or smash it. That's going to be nothing but no good."

Niles stares out over the groves to the east. In the night sky, Jupiter glows like a blue spark in Scorpio's lower claw. "Once it's happened," he tells Lila, "there's no way to smash it. If I can do it then someone else can do it, this decade, next decade, maybe not for twenty years, but it will happen. And this is only the beginning. As long as it's mine," he says, "I should use it."

"Jesus," Lila says softly, "I think you're getting in over your head. Don't you think things are fucked up enough already?"

"We'll see," Niles says, "I guess we'll see."

That night Lila refuses to sleep in the bedroom unless Niles removes the batteries from the device and leaves it out in the kitchen. She is already in bed when Niles returns from the kitchen and she says nothing and Niles sits at his bench to finish a page of notes.

Finally Lila turns over in bed and sighs. "I keep thinking about it," she says. "It's got to have a name. You made it, you name it. What are you going to call it?"

Niles stares at the quadrangle ruling of his notebook. A series of names, Greek and Latin, simple and complex, the detritus of formal education, runs through his head. "I call it what it is," he says at last. "It's a mindfogger."

Lila is lying on her back, staring at the ceiling, her

hair dark brown against the pillow. "The last privacy we've got left is inside our heads," she says. "When that's gone, then what?"

"I don't know," Niles says, and he is silent for a long time. "I guess there's only one way to find out."

"You're going to do it tomorrow?"

"First thing," Niles says. "Very first thing."

In the morning, while they are still in bed, the apartment quiet, the sun already bright, Lila tries to talk Niles out of taking the mindfogger to the factory. He should take another day, she tells him, to consider it.

Niles shakes his head and stretches. "Today is as good as tomorrow."

Lila is silent for a moment. "If it looks like there's going to be trouble," she says, "don't do it."

"I'm careful," Niles says. "I'm a champion taker of care."

"No you're not," Lila says. "This whole idea isn't careful at all."

"There won't be any trouble."

Lila looks doubtful, but she says nothing more. She cooks eggs for breakfast and makes up a lunch, and as she is putting it in his lunchbox, Niles tells her to leave a little extra room, about so big, and she glances up and nods. While Delores is in the living room, Niles takes the mindfogger down from the kitchen shelf and nestles the small aluminum case between two sandwiches in the lunchbox. On top he puts a screwdriver from his workbench. Lila watches this operation in silence and then she shakes her head. "You're really going to do it," she says.

"Maybe I won't," Niles says. "I'll see how I feel when I get there." He says this for Lila because he already knows exactly how he will feel. He is high on the idea and will only get higher.

Lila stands close to Niles and runs her hand down the faded blue sleeve of his shirt. She is wearing a white terry-cloth robe tied loosely at her middle, and her feet are bare and brown on the kitchen linoleum. She rests her forehead against his shoulder. "I love you," she says, "so be careful."

"I'll be fine," Niles says. "Don't even think about it."

Lila opens her mouth to say something more, but then Delores begins growling from the living room. "Let's go," she says, "time to hit the road." Lila walks down to the front porch with Niles and kisses him good-bye and Delores sighs, "Ain't love beautiful." As they drive away, Lila continues to stand on the porch, leaning against the wooden railing, and she watches the old Ford, burning oil, disappear into the increasing heat of the day.

When they arrive at the factory it is ten to eight. Delores goes up to the front office and Niles carries his lunchbox past the refrigerator where he usually leaves it, past assembly and electrolyte and shipping to a small rest room in the middle of the plant. As nearly as Niles has been able to determine, this is almost exactly the center of the factory. He locks himself in and opens his lunchbox and takes out the screwdriver. Up near the high white ceiling, a metal vent plate covers the mouth of a heating duct and by standing on a urinal Niles can just reach it. He removes the four screws from the metal grill and gently pulls it off so that the open mouth of the heating duct gapes in the tiled wall. The duct is cool, and Niles is certain it is never used.

He jumps down from the top of the urinal and takes the mindfogger from his lunchbox. The aluminum chassis is cold in his hands, smooth and solid and hard. The gain is now set as high as possible, and Niles figures that this will just cover the area of the plant. The batteries, freshly charged, will be good for months.

He stands on the urinal again, and holds the vent grill and the four screws and the screwdriver in one hand, and the mindfogger in the other. He sets the mindfogger inside the aluminum duct, pushed back a short distance, and he rests his finger on the tiny red microswitch. Once he presses the switch he will have to concentrate very hard to get the grill screwed back on correctly. He will have to concentrate very hard, and he tries to tighten his thinking like the flexion of a muscle. He fixes the moves in his mind, lifts the grill up almost to the duct, and then he presses the switch.

At eleven o'clock, the president of the company cancels his reservation at the golf course. It is his regular golf day, but he will have to visit the plant instead. Approaching retirement, he has lately made it a general principle not to go down before noon, but today appears to require an exception. An oddly garbled telephone call from the plant manager has informed him that production for the first three hours of the working day has dropped to an unprecedented zero units. The president is a man not unfamiliar with difficulty: he has a wife who will soon make local headlines by swallowing her barbiturates with gin, a son who has left business school to sing and dance in a gay theatrical troupe, a fine home built on fill that slides a foot downhill each rainy season. The president worries about the things he owns and the people he owns, his heart, his liver, his potency, the pace of the times, the fluctuations of the market, and now he has to worry about what is happening to his factory as well. But by the time he reaches his desk, he finds his long-nurtured talent for worry strangely diluted.

He sits in his paneled office, thick draperies drawn against the morning sun, sound hushed by the plush carpeting, and he spreads his hands over the heavy walnut surface of the desk and tries to remember what he was going to say. His mind seems to be working very slowly and it is a long time before he pulls the sentence together. "I want to know what is happening down there," he tells his vice-president-in-charge-of-production.

"I want to know what is happening down there," the vice-president-in-charge-of-production tells the plant manager.

"I want to know what is happening down there," the plant manager tells the foreman.

The foreman has just come from the production line but he will be damned if he can remember what was happening there. He will have to go down and look again.

By eleven, Boyd has managed to get the big paint-drying furnace started up. It has never taken him so long before, not even when he was first hired, but today he just keeps on turning the wrong valves and watching the wrong gauges until finally he blows out two burners by lighting them incorrectly and then there are all these repairs to do and the repairs take a little longer than he expected.

"All right," Boyd says to Niles and the two sprayers when at last the furnace has reached its steady sullen roar, "let's get our asses moving, these cases is stacking up," although, in fact and quite myteriously, there do not seem to be any cases at all coming in on the line.

Even though the conveyor is barren and still, Niles takes his can of red enamel and the camel's-hair brush and goes to sit on the stool. He decides that he will wait patiently for the batteries to start their deliberate parade and then he will try hard to do his job right, although he is not entirely certain he will be able to manage it. He seems to be doing a great deal of daydreaming today, and it is hard to keep his mind on . . . He stares at the paint brush in his hand, the can of enamel. On crosses, he thinks. Right. Everything, he decides, is going very nicely.

"No," Boyd says. "Goddamnit, no." One of the sprayers, moving slowly, has started to pick up a pile of battery cases in one corner of the paint room and the pile of hollow aluminum cubes is swaying precariously. "Those is *done,* goddamn you," Boyd says. "Do these here on the conveyor." But first Boyd has to get the conveyor started. It is driven by a small electric motor but it is sometimes hard to start because the brushes are badly worn and today Boyd has a great deal of trouble. Niles comes over to help and the two sprayers stand nearby and offer conflicting advice, and finally the foreman walks in, pocket glittering with metal pens and pencils.

The foreman smiles broadly at the group around the conveyor motor. "Little slow-up today," he says amiably, hands in his pockets, benignly surveying the paint department. "Nothing serious, but a little slow-up. Front office is checking it out."

"Maintenance," Boyd says, punching buttons, flipping switches, still trying to start the reluctant conveyor, and there is a new trace of desperation in his voice. He looks at the clock on the wall: in another half-hour it will be lunchtime. "We got to have maintenance down here," he says. "Everything is fucking up."

The foreman nods his head with sympathy. "You know me, Boyd. I did fifteen years on the line and I know the problems you face."

"Maintenance," Boyd repeats, "we got to have maintenance."

"Right," the foreman says, "right. Let me see what I can do." Boyd and Niles and the two sprayers watch the foreman amble out of the paint department, and it is the last time they see him that day.

By lunchtime, Boyd is shaking his head and pacing

the floor, stopping occasionally to kick the little conveyor motor, because nothing is getting done and it is his responsibility and nobody else gives a damn and there isn't anything he can seem to do about it. Every move he attempts just makes things worse.

"Don't you-all give a shit?" he finally asks Niles and the sprayers.

Certainly, they agree, they all give a shit.

Boyd knows this is significant but he can't quite remember what it is they give a shit about. "Well," he says, and he sits on a stool in the corner and worries.

At lunch—which due to some confusion with the noon whistle lasts for nearly an hour and a half—Boyd talks to the other department heads and discovers that they aren't doing anything either and do not seem to be overly concerned. There is considerable safety in numbers, Boyd decides, and so after lunch, when the rest of the paint department manages to return, he tells them that some days you win and some days you lose and you can't let the management bastards grind you down, and having thus stated it, his mind is greatly eased, and he almost enjoys the afternoon.

By four the situation has reached a crisis stage, or would have reached a crisis stage, had it occurred to anyone to so deem it. The casting furnace in the lead department, more complex than the paint-drying furnace, has never been started successfully, although many attempts have been made. The acid department, by a massive effort, has managed to produce one batch of electrolyte, an odd color but otherwise apparently correct, but now there is no place to put it because someone, as yet unidentified, has driven the forklift into a wall and bent the forks and there is no way to bring a pallet of plastic acid bottles over to be filled. The assembly line ladies have spent the day standing about, discussing a variety of subjects and occasionally trying to assemble batteries from parts left over from the previous day's production run, although these constructive efforts are always foiled by lengthy but unconcerned arguments as to exactly how the batteries are supposed to go together. The total accomplishment of the shipping department has been to dump a pallet of fifty boxed batteries over the edge of the loading dock, ten feet down to the hard asphalt. In the paint department, Boyd gives up on starting the conveyor when he discovers that the compressors for the paint spray guns will not start either, because their breakers are tripped and no one can quite remember where the breakers are. He gets out some wide brushes and he and Niles and the two sprayers sit on the floor and paint the cases by hand and set them out in the sun to dry. By four o'clock they have sixteen cases painted. They are not perfect paint jobs, but they are definitely painted, and Boyd announces, with some relief, that if they can have twenty-five done by quitting time he will be fucking glad to call it a day.

In the front office, amid considerable confusion, everyone is aware that something is monstrously wrong, but no one is certain just how to handle it. Nobody in the front office is particularly eager to go down to the plant itself, because it is noisy and too bright and far too hot, so they rely on the foreman to act as liaison. But no one in the front office has seen the foreman since the middle of the morning, when he was reported to be driving a forklift at a high rate of speed in the vicinity of the shipping dock.

By three o'clock the president of the company has lost all interest in the proceedings and locked himself in his office with a copy of a men's magazine. The vice-president is not sure just what to do, so he spends the afternoon polishing the sample batteries in the lighted showcase in the lobby. The plant manager is slightly concerned, because it seems to him, after lengthy consideration, that with the disappearance of the foreman the weight of responsibility has fallen on his shoulders.

At last he makes the pilgrimage down the paneled corridors to the thick green metal door that closes off the factory section from the front office. He steps into the plant, expecting bright heat, ready to shield his ears against the hissing and rattling and pounding and grating that usually fills the air. But he finds it almost dead silent. Nothing is happening. Because none of the furnaces are running, the air is comfortably cool. Half of the big overhead lights have never been switched on, so there is a pleasant dimness. The plant manager has never seen such a nice factory and he spends a few hours just walking around to enjoy it, talking to people, stopping occasionally to watch a department head trying to figure what to do, and in general passing the time in a manner so relaxing that he does not remember that anything is supposed to be wrong, until the whistle blows at five o'clock and people begin to file past the time clock, and by then, of course, it is too late. The plant manager cannot recall ever spending such a pleasant day at the plant, and it will not be until he is on his way home that he begins to worry in earnest.

Sometime around five, Niles punches out, wandering through the cloud of confusion that has condensed around the time clock, and he starts to walk to the parking lot to meet Delores. The mindfog withdraws, gradually, imperceptibly, and when he is a few yards past the walls of the plant, a patchy recollection of the day begins to congeal uncertainly into memory.

He has done it. It has worked better than Niles had ever dared to hope. He has done it: stopped the factory with a weapon that he does not mind using on himself. The factory will not be repaired by any number of the most dedicated maintenance men. For the second time in two days, Niles feels the adrenalin rush of success, and his head is light, and he smiles at nothing in particular. These next few weeks, he is certain, will be the most interesting this factory has ever seen.

Halfway to the parking lot, hands in his pockets, he turns back to look at the big cement-block building, sharply shadowed by the late afternoon sun. His co-workers, in workshirts and khakis and stretchpants and windbreakers, continue to pass through the wide glass doors, blinking their eyes in the brightness of the sun. Boyd approaches him, walking slowly in his crumpled overalls. "See you tomorrow," Niles says to him.

Boyd looks at Niles, squinting, his wide face uncertain and faintly puzzled, as if in the bright sunshine he is slowly coming to some slightly numbing realizations. "Yep," he says briefly, and then he shakes his head. "Maybe tomorrow we better get something done."

"Sure," Niles says. "Fuck it, tomorrow's another day."

Boyd nods and frowns and walks off slowly.

Delores is already sitting in the car, the radio playing, and she looks as if she has been sitting there for some time. "Left early today," she says cheerfully out her window. "Just not anything to do, so we all left early."

Niles shakes his head as he gets into the car. He has already decided that he will tell Delores nothing. "Pretty strange day," he says tentatively, "wasn't it?"

Delores smiles as she starts the car. She is smiling with increasing frequency now, and Niles thinks it is working a permanent improvement in the contours of her face. "You noticed it too?" she asks. "Wasn't it"—she searches for the word—"wonderful?"

"Wonderful?" Niles repeats. "Well," he says, "it was sort of slow down on the line."

"That's it," Delores says. "It was slow. No panics, no rushing around, no loud talking. Just taking it easy." She nods as she turns her head to back the car out of the parking space. "Maybe it's because it's the first day of summer," she says. "Did you know that? I wish every day could be like today."

Niles rolls down his window, stretches his arm out into the air. "Who knows?" he says. "Maybe they can."

"All right," the speaker says when, at last, after lengthy fumblings, he has organized the mechanical aids for his presentation. "Who here is proud of his country?" It is eleven o'clock in the morning and the intense July sun has been completely shut out of the factory lunchrooms, now dim and cool and faintly illuminated by bright color slides projected on the screen behind the rented orator. His hair is curly, piled high on his head, like a model in a 1940's high school hygiene textbook. He wears a striped business suit and sways slightly on the folding speaker's platform, as if rocked by gentle waves. "I mean way deep down," he insists, "I want to know: who here is proud of his country? Let me see some hands."

Niles and Delores sit in the last row of metal chairs, closest to the door. Niles slouches down in his chair and puts his feet up on the seat in front of him. He is greatly impressed by this speaker's composure and presence of mind in the face of an audience so lazy and confused they might as well be made of melting wax. A rule he has formulated these last few weeks at the factory is that the less mind one has to begin with, the more difficult it is to fog.

The motivational research speaker grows increasingly insistent. "Let me see those hands," he says again. "I want to count, now let me see them. Who here is proud?"

Attendance is compulsory for the entire factory but
the event is ill timed. It is only an hour until lunch, and
lately many people have become accustomed to taking
short naps during this period. From one corner of the
room there is constant quiet snoring.

"Hands," the speaker reminds them once more, patiently, but now the slightest quaver appears in his rich
voice.

Niles realizes that the man will not go on until he
gets a response, so he raises his hand. The portion of
the audience still awake obediently raise their hands as
well. Sure, everyone is proud of his country. Why not?
Niles raises his hand higher. He thinks his country has
a nice shape.

"It makes me glad to see that," the speaker says with
relief, "it makes me very glad to see that." He tries to
explain why he is glad as the colorful slides projected
behind his back continue to change. The slides are
scenes of industrial America, steel workers and assembly line workers and construction workers photo-
graphed against the dramatic lighting of blast furnaces
or arc welders, frozen in vivid heroic Kodachromes,
changing automatically every ten seconds. The speaker
holds his manuscript tightly with both hands, fastening
his attention on it, pronouncing each word as if won at
great cost.

"I want to talk about tradition," he says slowly.
"The tradition of the American laboring man. I want
to talk about pride. The pride of American craftsman-
ship. I want to talk about . . ."

There is a long silence. After a few moments Niles
understands that the speaker has lost his place. He is a
five-hundred-dollar speaker, known in management
circles as a guaranteed boon to sagging production, an
old-style orator armed with modern technology who
can draw fire from the most passive of groups, and
now he has lost his place. The silence stretches on,

broken only by the regular automatic reflex of the slide projector, as the speaker stares baffled at his manuscript and the audience sits benignly patient.

"Jesus," the speaker says softly when he cannot find his place, "Jesus Christ." He sets his manuscript down and gazes out at the audience and the audience gazes back at him. He takes a few steps backward and knocks over the projection screen and sends the giant color images of American workers spilling across the floor and ceiling and walls of the lunchroom. The orator appears not to notice.

"What's he doing?" Delores asks Niles. "Is this part of it?"

Niles shrugs. "Wait and see."

Now the speaker cannot find where he has set his manuscript. In his search he wanders into the projector beam and is coated with bright shifting colors. Someone in the audience begins to applaud, and then others, thinking this signals the end of the talk, start to clap also. The speaker looks up and smiles. He steps down from the platform and walks slowly up the center aisle, still looking for his manuscript. He walks the full length of the aisle, searching the rows of folding chairs, and soon he is at the lunchroom door, and seeing the door, he opens it and walks out. While the door is still open, a few follow him. Everyone else continues to sit, watching the bright slides automatically project themselves across the room, a different straining back or sweating brow flashed every ten seconds across the coffee vending machine on the opposite wall.

"I don't get it," Delores says finally.

Niles shakes his head. The entire presentation has been most mysterious.

"Is it over?" Delores asks.

Niles considers the situation. "Sure," he says finally. "I guess so."

He and Delores go out in back and sit in the shade

of the vacant loading dock, watching the smog rise thick and yellow in the valley, until it is lunchtime. Technically they are missing work, but in reality, these days at the factory, it makes very little difference. At the other end of the loading dock the two college girls who work in assembly are sharing a joint, blue smoke drifting lazily across the empty pallets, the unused forklifts. Lately the loading dock has developed the atmosphere of a back proch.

"This factory," Delores says at last, "is pretty strange. I've never seen anything as strange as this factory before." It is something she says every day, in one way or another, as if she feels a regular need to register her perception of reality with the outside world, and Niles will always tell her yes, she is right, it is very strange. "It's nice, though," Delores hastens to add, "it's strange but it's sort of nice, you know what I mean?" and Niles agrees again: yes, he thinks, he knows exactly what she means.

For two weeks now the mindfogger has cast its delicately relentless electromagnetic spell over the assembled minds of the battery factory, and for two weeks the factory has operated as if cursed. If anything can go wrong, it does go wrong, and each new disaster is met with agreeable nodding resignation on the part of everyone involved.

One morning the floor of the electrolyte department is flooded with concentrated acid, and the entire department is abandoned for three days. Another morning five hundred pounds of molten lead somehow escapes from the casting furnace and leaves huge shiny leaden lava flows on the concrete factory floor. In the paint department, the nozzle of a spray gun becomes clogged and before anyone notices, the compressor line blows apart and the burst rubber hose, flopping wildly, wraps itself around Boyd's bulk like a python in spastic ecstasy. Remarkably, there are no serious injuries:

even the workers who figure in spectacular forklift col-
lisions are invariably loose and relaxed and thus un-
harmed. A large illustrated sign is placed over the time
clock, with careful instructions regarding the proper
use of time cards, but it does little good. Cards are
stamped upside down and backwards, at apparently
random times of the day, traded back and forth so that
sometimes a single card is stamped by seven or eight
different people.

None of this happens on purpose: everyone wants to
do right and tries to do right, but it just doesn't work
out. For the two-week period, production averages
47.3 batteries a day, with an eighty percent failure
rate. Most of the batteries turned out are almost totally
handmade, and show it.

"We took a nose dive," becomes a phrase ritually repeated in conversation. It is a concept introduced into
currency by the foreman, who, following his mysterious disappearance on the first mindfogged day has
since circulated faithfully through the factory, each
morning trying to get things started, each afternoon
trying to shut things down. He maintains a sense of humor about the situation and, at least while in the factory, is often sighted laughing and shaking his head,
shaking his head and laughing. Rumor connects him
with the unexplained forklift damages the first day, and
in fact he will no longer drive one of the rapidly deteri-
orating machines. He and Niles have several fine, ram-
bling conversations about Niles' plans for the future,
which the foreman hopes include the battery factory,
and Niles assures him repeatedly that the factory is in
fact already very much in his plans.

Niles goes to work each morning with a growing
sense of wonder at the implications of what he has
done; Delores, with bright anticipation of the day
ahead. Although Lila is pleased that the experiment
has not already proven disastrous, she cannot imagine

what the mindfogged factory is like, and Niles finds it difficult to describe, but soon changes are obvious even at home.

"She's almost stopped drinking," Lila tells Niles one night after a week or so has passed. "Have you noticed that? She hardly drinks at all." Previously Delores would spend several evenings a week sewing, which meant that she would drag a half-stitched ball of cloth out of the closet and sit in the living room and listen to music and drink gin, or sometimes vodka, and by the end of the evening it would always be a tossup whether she had advanced or lost ground on her unidentifiable sewing project. Now, however, she appears truly to sew, smiling and cheerful and plainly stone-sober. She is, these days, rarely morose. In the mornings she reads only the sports section. Niles finds this, and many other effects of the mindfogger, as yet quite inexplicable, and each evening he fills pages of his notebook with observations and theories. There is much he does not understand. "At least," Lila tells him as he writes, "you may be saving a liver."

But, as Niles has known from the beginning, such a thing cannot go on for long without attracting undesirable attention. Each afternoon he watches the big delivery trucks pull away from the factory, almost empty, often containing only a dozen batteries where once they hauled thousands. The Morton factory, by virtue of its previously exemplary efficiency, holds the exclusive contract for military storage batteries, and it is not long before, all over the vast American empire, motor pools and airplane hangars and garages and maintenance shops begin to run short of packaged electricity. There are large stockpiles of batteries secreted in a hundred places around the globe, like the caches of a hyperactive ground squirrel; but a nation that wishes to stay Number One must think far ahead, and soon supply officers and parts-men and warehousers all over the world are sending out puzzled inquiries as to exactly where all the batteries have gone.

In less than a week there are small groups of suit-coated gentlemen wandering through the plant, loosely directed by the foreman or plant manager, appearing suitably baffled by their surroundings yet still radiating authority. Steps must be taken to repair this errant factory. Niles quickly divines the reasoning behind these steps: a factory is like any other machine, the thinking goes, and in order to repair it, a replacement or refashioning of parts is all that is required. The only difficulty, of course, is that in a factory, certain of the critically interlocking parts happen to be organic and conscious.

On the fourth day the front office brings in a team of doctors from Los Angeles, and there are medical checkups for everyone in the plant, conducted in the first-aid room. Samples of the air, and the water, and the food on the lunchwagon are sent out to a laboratory for painstaking analysis. During the mornings in the lunchroom certain psychological tests are administered to randomly selected employees by an industrial psychologist who accompanies the doctors. Niles is given one of these tests and he thinks very carefully and answers questions carefully and even so is quickly confused.

"I want you to tell me which of these shapes are most nearly the same," the psychologist says to Niles, reading from a printed script, and then he holds up a big piece of cardboard with five colorful shapes on it.

"None of them," Niles says after lengthy deliberation.

"No," the psychologist explains, "two of them have to be. It's made that way."

"None of them," Niles repeats. "Look for yourself."

The psychologist looks for himself. He looks for a long time, checks the answer key, looks again, plainly puzzled.

"Maybe you're holding it upside down," Niles says.

The psychologist frowns.

"Maybe you're too close," Niles suggests. "Let me hold it for you."

The psychologist shakes his head. "Give me a chance to think." He stares at the shapes, and Niles gives him a chance to think.

"Let's do the next one," the psychologist says finally. It takes them two and a half hours to do the fifteen-minute test and by the time it is finished, the only person more confused than Niles is the psychologist. Niles offers to stay and help with the next one but the psychologist says he will try to handle it himself. Boyd is the next subject, and his test takes four hours.

In the end, after much clinical and chemical scrutiny, the factory is found to be in perfect health, the environment is declared to be positively nontoxic, and some previously recorded cases of chronic hypertension and migraine are even noted to have disappeared. These results are posted on a bulletin board and are met with much enthusiasm and pride. "No goddamned excuses!" becomes the foreman's new salutation, and the factory throws itself into work with redoubled effort. Production does not increase.

The front office, after several lengthy and generally unprofitable think-sessions, comes to conclude that they are faced with some sort of strange and unprecedented guerrilla-style tactic of organized labor, most likely imported from overseas, that involves no obvious threats or demands. "Insidious," the president terms it in a memo. "A threat to the foundation of all labor-management relations." The second week commences with a series of stiff warnings. An angry and emotional letter signed by both the president and the plant manager appears on the bulletin board in place of the medical report. *Many of us,* the letter begins, *have worked together, built together, dreamed together, since the day this plant first opened its doors.* The letter pulls no punches. Portions of it are repeatedly quoted at lunch.

Each department head is individually brought up to the front office for a short talk in the president's suite. Changes may have to be made, they are told, if production does not increase, and immediately. The front office has tried to be patient but there are limits to patience and steps may be taken. Production must increase, each head is told, straight from the shoulder— no nonsense, no guff, no room for slackers or laggards. Each department head is eager to comply. All heads agree that they would truly like to see the factory get back on its feet. Boyd returns from the interview close to tears and gives the paint department a heartfelt reaming. The scene is repeated all over the plant. Production does not increase.

Then there are promises, delivered on mimeographed sheets for each department head to read to his department. There will be a round of fine bonuses in the next paycheck envelope if the factory will just get to work. There will be an all-expenses-paid weekend for two in Las Vegas for each department head, there will be contests in which workers may win new compact cars or color television sets or well-stocked freezers, there will be all of these things and perhaps even more if only production will increase. And still nothing.

At last there are few alternatives to a mass firing, but this is a step no one in the front office wishes to initiate. To dismiss the majority of one's employees is a relatively bald statement of executive failure that will doubtless be remembered when the time for contract renewals rolls around. Instead, the plant manager, inspired, schedules the series of expensive motivational lectures—a series which lasts a total of fifteen befuddled minutes.

On the loading dock, after the lecture, Delores shakes her head again. "I heard this morning that they might shut the factory down," she says. "Can they do that?"

Niles shrugs. "Don't worry," he says. "Nobody knows what's going to happen."

Nobody—and least of all Niles. It is clearly his move again. The factory has maintained a remarkable and glorious level of disorder for two full weeks, but Niles is not certain it can continue much longer. Lila feels even more strongly about it. "You should get it out of there," she tells him every night now. "It's only a matter of time before they take that factory apart."

Niles knows this is most likely true. The mindfogger will not be detected by any conventional equipment sensitive to electromagnetic radiation, but each time he walks into the rest room in the center of the factory, his own eyes are drawn irresistibly to the heating duct that hides the device, and perhaps, he thinks, other eyes are as well. Sometimes he imagines that he can see a flash of naked aluminum through the metal grating. It is a vulnerable place to leave a device of such power.

"And how long until the government starts to investigate the factory?" Lila asks him relentlessly in the evenings. "How long until they run a check on all the employees? I bet they're doing it right now. Jesus," she says, "you're going to get fucked."

"Oh," Niles says easily, "it's—"

"No," Lila insists, "this whole thing is just too weird. Haven't you done enough? What's the point of sticking around?"

"It's an experiment," Niles says, "there's still—"

"What you're doing," Lila tells him, "is making a fucked-up system even more fucked-up. What good is that? How does that make you happier?"

Niles recognizes the symptoms that he has seen build for weeks: Lila is growing discontented with life in Morton. She wants to go north, to get away from civilization—to practice her moves, he figures, for the apocalypse, before Niles manages to drag her into his own private disaster. "Just a little longer," Niles tells her. "Then we'll travel. The rest of what I have to do I can do with pencil and paper."

Lila shakes her head. "All right," she agrees. "A little longer."

Today, in the comfortable shade of the unused loading dock, Niles at last decides that it has been long enough. It is time to get the mindfogger out of the factory. The lecture was a pathetic effort, but it was an effort of desperate thinking, of men with their backs to an unseen wall bringing in a rival sorcerer, with colored lights and incantations, to combat the effects of a spell they can never hope to break themselves. Their next efforts could be much more serious, and the risk is all Niles'.

Tomorrow he will take the mindfogger home with him. The experiment is over. So is this portion of his life, because he cannot stay on at the factory when it begins to operate again. He has money in the bank; he and Lila can head north. There will be better places to spend their energy.

"I love this factory," Delores says, as the noon whistle begins to blow. "I mean I really like to come here. I don't want them to close it down."

The noon whistle jams, continues to blow, a long banshee wailing that gives no sign of stopping. Niles stands up and brushes off the seat of his pants. The whistle goes on, an unbroken shrill cry, and Niles smiles at Delores and helps her get up. "They won't close it," Niles tells her over the scream of the whistle. "Don't worry. This factory will be here just as long as you want to stay."

They go inside the factory, and the whistle, its relay jammed, apparently irreparable, screeches through the first five minutes of lunch, until at last the foreman climbs a ladder and smashes it with a wrench, and the screech turns to a whistle, slides to a whimper, and rasps, at last, into silence.

That afternoon, after work, as soon as Niles opens the door to the stairwell, he knows that something is different in the apartment. Delores, right behind him, notices nothing, but Niles senses a difference just at the edge of his perception: it is something in the air, he thinks, or something in the way his footsteps echo up the stairs, or simply something in his head, but as soon as he reaches the top of the stairs he is certain. In the kitchen, bread and cheese and sardines and two cans of beer are set out on the table, and sitting at the table are Lila and someone Niles has never seen before.

Lila, wearing faded cut-off jeans and a white halter top, gets up and hugs Niles and kisses him. She tastes of oily sardines. "Niles," Lila says, "this is Albert."

Albert. Niles stares. Lila has never said much about Albert. "Very exploitative," she told Niles once, "but also very loving." Niles told her that sounded like something of a contradiction. "Oh no," Lila told him then. "They go together perfectly."

Albert stands up. He is taller than Niles, with long blond hair neatly styled, and a pale narrow face with prominent cheekbones that lend him a faintly cadaverous appearance. His dress shirt has been newly pressed and his slacks are of some smooth glossy synthetic material. "Glad to meet you," Albert says heartily, and they shake hands. "Lila's been telling me all about you."

"Nice meeting you," Niles says, and he goes over to the refrigerator and gets a beer as Lila introduces Delores to Albert. Niles is instantly hostile. He does not like how close Albert is sitting to Lila, he does not like the way Albert dresses or the feel of his handshake, and as a general rule he does not trust people who are taller than he. Niles wonders what Lila could possibly have seen in this character. It is almost as if he is now also viewing some new, recently turned side of Lila.

Niles cuts a piece of cheese and sits in the only empty chair, across from Lila.

"Albert just stopped by to see how I was doing," Lila says.

Albert smiles at Niles. "I've been looking for Lila for a month," he says. "You did a pretty good job of disappearing."

Not good enough, Niles thinks. "Well, you found us," Niles says, and he pauses. "Why don't you stay for dinner?"

"Thank you," Albert says, nodding his head. He is boning each of his sardines with a fork.

Niles takes another bit of cheese and then he looks through the kitchen door into the living room and sees the suitcase. It is as stylish as Albert's clothes, with brushed aluminum trim and a sleek shape. Niles looks at Albert again. "Your suitcase?"

Albert begins to nod and then Lila breaks in. "Albert's going to stay with us for a few days," she says brightly.

Niles stares at her. "Oh yeah?"

"I'm moving out of southern California," Albert says. "I've got a few days, so I just thought I'd—"

"He can sleep in the living room," Lila tells Niles. "It'll be nice to have some company."

"Sure," Niles says, "fine," but in fact he does not think this is fine at all. He swallows the last fragment of cheese, wipes his mouth. "I'll go change my shirt," he says, and he looks at Lila. "Make myself presentable for company." He goes into the bedroom, and Lila excuses herself and follows him.

"What the hell do you think you're doing?" Niles says as soon as Lila closes the bedroom door. "Don't you think this is going to get a little tense?"

Lila stands in front of him and starts to unbutton Niles' shirt. "Come on," she says quietly. "He needs a place to stay."

Niles shakes his head. "So let him stay in a motel. He could hock that fancy suitcase and have money for a year."

"Don't talk so loud," Lila says, "and besides, it's not money. He's always had plenty of money. He's lonely, that's all. He needs people around."

"And you're going to keep him company. Real generous of you."

"Don't be like that," Lila says, and she slips the shirt over Niles' shoulders and pulls off one sleeve, then the other. "Come on, it's all right."

"Listen," Niles says, shrugging off the shirt. "How do you think I'm going to feel, having him hanging around?"

"You're jealous," Lila says, smiling.

"Damn right," Niles says. "Is that what you want?"

"No," says Lila. "You shouldn't be jealous. There's nothing to be jealous about."

Niles shakes his head. He does not like to think that Lila slept with Albert, that she lived with him, that she cooked for him, that his was the first face she saw every morning. Lila is now such a part of his life that he can barely credit the notion that at one time she was part of another's. It is nearly incomprehensible.

She brings him a clean shirt, smiling, trying to make Niles smile too. The Morton sun has bleached long streaks in her hair the color of maple wood. "Besides," she says, "I think Delores could use a little company. What do you think?"

Niles shrugs. Perhaps he is being unreasonable. "Fuck it," he says, "okay."

Lila hugs him and scrapes her fingernails very gently down his bare back. "You have to help people who are down," she says. "Because sure as shit someday you'll be down yourself."

"And then I can go stay with Albert?" Niles says sullenly.

"Or something," Lila says. "Or something."

That night Lila cooks a large dinner, and before they eat, she changes into a skirt and a thin top with a low neck. She wears a nice perfume and, in the kitchen, when Albert and Delores are out in the living room, Niles pulls her hair. "Who you trying to impress?" he asks her, half-joking.

"Nobody," Lila says, but Niles knows this is not the case. She is proving something to someone, making something manifest. She balances the forces in her life with a neat, aesthetic skill.

At dinner the talk ranges over a variety of superficial subjects and Niles concludes that Albert is pleasant enough, if not particularly bright, although he still cannot understand what it is that attracted Lila to him. He decides that he probably wouldn't really want to know. Albert seems to have a considerable knowledge of economics, and he and Delores discuss at great length the financial condition of the country. It is as animated as Niles has seen Delores for some time, and soon, when the bottle of wine is nearly empty, everyone is talking freely.

"Where are you moving?" Niles asks Albert.

Albert drinks carefully from his glass. "I'm moving

north," he says. "I'm buying an interest in a cattle ranch."

"Ooh," Delores says, "that sounds very interesting."

Albert shrugs, looks at Lila across the table. "It seems to me like the best place to put your money these days."

Niles nods. "Sounds good," he says, "sounds very nice," although somehow, Albert as a rancher is an image that simply refuses to form. Niles has difficulty visualizing Albert doing anything much more rigorous than lacing his high shiny boots.

"It's something permanent," Albert says. "It's something secure."

"I admire that," Delores says. "That's really going out and making a place for yourself."

Albert shrugs again, modestly. Lila gazes down into her empty dessert bowl. Niles pours himself more wine.

When the table has been cleared, Niles and Albert go out and sit in the living room. Albert asks if he can turn the television on.

"Sure," Niles says, "go ahead."

Albert turns the picture on and leaves the sound off. The picture appears to be an old war movie with a German prison camp commandant who vaguely resembles Albert. "You don't want to turn the sound on?" Niles asks.

Albert shakes his head. "You know," he says, "just something to keep us company." He leans over and examines the picture closely, as if warming his hands at the mouth of a potbellied stove. "Listen," he says to Niles after a minute. "Lila is only part of the reason I came out here."

"She's enough of a reason," Niles says.

"True," Albert agrees, "true. But I wanted to meet you, too."

"I'm flattered," says Niles, warily.

"That day Lila left me," Albert says, "that day the cops came to my apartment, they asked me a lot of questions about you."

Niles nods, not surprised. "And all you could tell them was that you thought I'd stolen your woman."

Albert shrugs. "They already had that figured out. All they wanted to know about was gadgets."

"Gadgets?" Niles tries to look his most puzzled.

"You know," Albert says, "electronic devices. Inventions. Gadgets."

Niles decides there is an ominous drift to this conversation. "That was a bad bust," he says, confidentially, one freak to another. "The cat was dealing cocaine, very big quantities. Lila and I were lucky to get out."

Albert fixes him with an unswerving stare. "It must be very interesting being an inventor," he says. "It must give you a real sense of purpose."

"Shit," Niles says, "I fix a few TV's, a few radios, I'm working up to a second-class license, I stay pretty busy but I don't do much interesting. All I want to do is get out of that factory, set up my own shop or something, be my own boss."

Albert acts as if he has heard nothing. "I've been wondering what kind of stuff you're working on. If you have any gadgets you think would sell, I think maybe I could find financing and start a little production company. You get a nicer slice of the pie that way than if you just sell rights to one of the big boys."

Niles admires Albert's persistence. People always seem to turn up who want to help him look out for his own best interests. "Well," he says, "if I think of anything I'll let you know. It's a very generous offer."

"I mean," Albert continues, again as if Niles has said nothing, "you guys are the guys who make the world these days, if you know what I mean." He points to the silent television, the stereo, the electric lights, a clock radio in the corner. "And cars. And airplanes. And *drugs,* for god's sake. All of these things. These days the guy who makes the new gadget makes the history. He turns everybody's head around whether they want it turned around or not. Let me tell you: it is the business to be in."

"Sounds great," Niles says, "just great."

Albert nods. "Hell of a lot easier than sweating your ass off in some lousy factory. Tell me what you're working on, and we could look into the possibilities. I think it could be very easily done."

Niles shakes his head. "I don't think I've got anything that would sell."

"Hey," Albert says, smiling, "don't bullshit me. I can see that workbench back in your bedroom. I know the questions the cops asked me. You've got a product, I can tell that a mile away. Sitting on it's going to do you no good at all."

"I've got nothing," Niles says, "and even if I did it probably wouldn't be for sale. There's too many products already." He shakes his head: "Listen: new tools do exactly the same thing as old tools, fill the same needs, maybe faster or neater or in greater quantity, but the same needs. Tools don't turn heads, man, they only give the impression they have. If people can keep buying new tools in fancier boxes then they'll never stop to think what they used the old ones for."

"All right," Albert says, "all right," but now he is very serious and choosing his words with care. "Let's not talk about products. Let's talk about needs, that's your word. Listen to what I've got to say: this country is falling apart. Your need, my need, everybody's need right now is survival. Some of us just happen to see it more clearly than others. Ten years from now, when you have to wear an oxygen mask to go outside, when you have to drop halazone in your tap water before you can drink it, when you can't go outdoors after dark without a gun and a spare clip, when you leave your apartment overnight and come back and find that somebody else has moved in, then let me tell you what your need is going to be." He pauses for a moment, catches his breath, speaks very quietly. "You're going to want land. Fifty acres surrounded by wilderness, a deep well, arable soil, some livestock. Self-sufficiency. Some place you can take Lila and know that you can live like human beings, and make babies and know they can live like human beings too. That's what I'm doing, that's what you should be doing. That's what any thinking person should be doing today. And do you know how?"

Niles, numbed by the flow of words, shakes his head.

"Money," Albert says. "Bread. That's all it takes. One good product. But we've got to do it now. Before the rush begins, before everyone else realizes it, before we get trampled in the stampede."

Niles smiles briefly. "You mean we need time to put up our fences."

"Exactly," Albert says. "Exactly."

The silence in the living room stretches on. On the television the prison camp commandant is lecturing a parade ground full of tattered prisoners. At last Niles shakes his head. "No," he says. "You may be right about the future, I've thought the same myself, but even if I had a product, I wouldn't give it to you. You haven't thought it through. Exploited technology is what you're trying to escape. You're trying to get out of a burning building by lighting matches."

"Wrong," Albert says, "wrong, wrong, wrong," and then Lila and Delores walk in from the kitchen. For an instant, involuntarily, Niles imagines Lila standing in some wooden farm kitchen, beside a hand water pump, peeling vegetables they have grown themselves. No electricity, no cars, no television, no factories.

"Hey," Lila says, "what's going on in here?"

Niles shrugs. "We're talking about the future."

Lila makes a face and sits on the couch next to Niles, folding her legs beneath herself. "Oh," she says, "let's talk about something cheerful instead."

When Niles and Lila finally go to bed, they leave Albert and Delores in the living room, watching television. Niles feels as tightly tensed as spring steel, and he barely listens to Lila as they get ready for bed.

"Don't you think Albert and Delores look alike?" Lila is saying.

"Nope," Niles says. "Huh-uh."

"You don't?"

Niles shakes his head, tapping the surface of his workbench, staring fixedly at the bright poster on the wall.

"People used to say that Albert and I sort of looked alike."

Niles looks at her. "Talk about something else."

"Well, they did."

"Well, you don't."

Lila gets into bed, pulls the sheet over herself. "You're in a good mood tonight."

Niles shrugs. "I've got a lot to think about."

Lila says nothing, sighs, yawns. "Niles," she says finally, quietly, "Albert asked me to move up to his farm for a while. Just to work. He needs hands."

Niles stares at the surface of his workbench and his stomach clenches like a fist. Losing Lila to her fears of the future has been a possibility in the back of his mind for a long time. "Well," he says carefully, "that's great. That's always what you wanted. A farm."

"Yeah," Lila says, "right."

Niles says nothing for a moment. He pushes a stray resistor with the tip of his finger. "You going to do it?"

Lila moves her head on the clean white pillowcase,

is silent for a long time. "I guess not," she says finally.

Niles nods. "Why not?"

She turns her head to look at Niles. "Because I'm an idiot, I guess."

Niles smiles, nods again. There is a stretch of silence. "Well," he says, "I'm glad." He pauses. "I'm going to take the mindfogger out of the factory tomorrow. In a week or so I'll quit the job. We can go to the mountains then, if you still want to."

"Great," Lila says, raising up on her elbows to look at Niles, "that's great. It's about time."

"Sure," Niles says, "great." He shakes his head. "In another week the factory will be like it was," he says. "Like nothing happened."

"It was an experiment," Lila says. "Just a test. You'll do it again, sometime, somewhere, or you'll make a lot of them, or something."

"Or something," Niles repeats. He sits at his bench, pushes the tools aside, leans forward, his head in his hands. He tries to imagine his mind as the surface of a clear still pond, mirrorlike, without a ripple, but he cannot hold the image. Too much inside his head now, too much to worry about, too many separate ideas: Lila and Albert, Delores and Albert, the mindfogger, the factory, his work, the future—Albert's picture of the future sticks in his mind like gristle between the teeth—all of these things combine to cast a persistent film of anxiety over his vision like grease on a windshield.

He knows this feeling: the anxiety of the nonspecific threat; an overdose of civilization. Maybe Lila is right, maybe it is time to head for the mountains and sit in a tree and not think until his head clears out again. In primal nature, the threats are finite and regular and familiar: drought, flood, fire, animals, the cold, your nearest hostile neighbor. In technological society the threats have grown diffuse—each one smaller but the total number greatly multiplied—and now the confluence of threats chips away at the quality of life from a thousand different directions. Unwelcome visitors with unwelcome ideas, parking tickets, bad food off a caterer's truck, each event quite trivial; but the sum total of these events builds, inevitably, to that odd and anxious feeling that somewhere, somehow, things are going very wrong.

Niles touches the tools on his bench, idly stacks the papers and notebooks all to one side. "Come to bed," Lila says, and this time Niles nods.

His head feels as heavy as if cast from lead as he lays it on the pillow next to Lila.

"It's okay," Lila says, "it's okay, it's okay," and for the moment it is, and Niles holds her and sleeps.

In the morning, Albert rises with the rest of them and corners Niles in the hallway and asks him again about gadgets and products. Niles is carrying the screwdriver he will take to the plant in order to retrieve the mindfogger.

"No," Niles tells him, slipping the screwdriver in his back pocket. "Period. Not interested. Someday if I have a good idea maybe I'll get in touch, okay?"

Albert looks at him for a long time. "Sure," he says, "suit yourself." He smiles, but shakes his head. "It's up to you."

They eat breakfast and then Niles goes back in the bedroom to get ready for work. Lila comes in and sits on the bed. "Be careful today," she says.

"This is the easy part," Niles tells her. "It's all downhill from here."

"Just be careful," Lila says, "all right?"

"Sure," says Niles, and he starts out of the bedroom toward the kitchen. As he is passing by the stairwell he hears a light knocking at the front door. No one else hears it, so he goes down the stairs and opens the door.

Two short-haired men in coats and ties, one tall and one shorter, with a heavy build, are standing on the front porch. Instantly Niles knows what is happening. He takes a step backward and his heel hits the bottom stair.

"Niles Spindrift," the taller man says as he pulls a leather wallet from his breast pocket and displays his identification. "FBI. There's a warrant out for your arrest on a federal charge of draft evasion plus counts of illegal flight to avoid arrest and grand theft auto. You'll have to come with us." The man closes his identification case and reaches one hand into his coat pocket and there is a clink of metal on metal. Niles takes another step back, up onto the first stair.

The shorter man takes a small black automatic pistol from a shoulder holster. "Step out here," he says. Niles looks at the gun and steps out onto the porch. They lean him, spreadeagled, against the wall of the house and pat him down and empty his pockets, firmly, neatly, efficiently. One of them examines the screwdriver from his back pocket with care.

"Wait a minute," Niles says, "what the hell is this?"

The shorter man grabs him by one arm and pulls him to his feet. "Stick your hands out."

"Listen," Niles begins, and then the taller man pushes him once, hard, so that he falls back and hits the wall of the house.

"Stick your hands out," the shorter man repeats, and Niles sticks his hands out and there is another clink of metal as they handcuff him.

One on each side, they start to walk Niles down the porch steps and out to an unmarked white car parked at the curb. The door to the apartment is still open. "Wait," says Niles, "let me tell—"

"You'll have a phone call," the tall man says, keeping a hard constant pressure on Niles' arm.

They open the back door of the car and put Niles in.

The back doors have no inside handles, and a steel screen separates the front and back seats. The two men get in the front seat and the short one starts the engine while the tall one turns around to look at Niles through the steel screen. "Niles," he says, not unkindly, "I think you're screwed. Let me tell you your rights."

Outside the morning is already warm and clear and perfect. Each summer day in Morton mimics the previous, predicts the next, as if imprinted with the regularity of the assembly line. Niles does not listen to the quickly droned recitation from the front seat. He stares, quite vacantly, his mind empty of thought, his stomach shot with adrenalin, and as the car picks up speed, the old houses flash by in the windows, framed by telephone poles, like a long strip of movie film in unsynchronized time.

Before the unmarked car reaches the freeway, one agent radios ahead to make arrangements. They will take Niles to the county jail, located at the barren outskirts of Santa Teresa, ten miles to the west of Morton. Niles sees no point in saying anything, so he remains silent during the ride through town. When asked if he understands his rights he nods his head and continues to stare out the window. He understands his rights well enough to know he should take a good look at the world.

The county jail is a big square two-story building of whitewashed stucco, like an immense sugar cube in the bright morning sun. The agents take Niles in through a side entrance into a small ceiling-high cage with an electrically operated door. The door opens and closes with a solenoid that, while activated, buzzes like a nest of wasps. Through the electrical door and down a short flight of concrete steps is the center corridor of the main cellblock, cement walls painted pale green, housing the barbershop and a supply room and the booking room and a holding cell. A dusty blackboard on one wall has chalked-in prisoner totals: 110 women and 284 men. "They do a good business here," Niles says to one of the agents, who ignores him.

A fat deputy waddles slowly from the booking room and unlocks the barred door of the holding cell. The taller agent takes the handcuffs off Niles and returns them to his suitcoat and the deputy locks Niles into the cell. "When can I see a lawyer?" Niles asks, but the agents and the deputy turn away.

The holding cell is just about the size of the first aid room at the factory. Wooden benches are bolted to two walls, and there are an open toilet and a small sink on the wall opposite the barred door. The floor slants slightly to a drain in one corner and it needs hosing down. Against one wall sit two Mexican nationals, neither looking older than eighteen, wearing high-heeled shiny leather zip-up boots and tight sharkskin slacks. On the other wall sprawls an old man dressed in yellow jail coveralls, his face grey and black-stubbled and his head half-shaven to reveal a wide stitched wound high on his pink scalp. He wears handcuffs and leg chains, and the moment the cell door closes he looks at Niles. "Cigarette?" he says. "You got a cigarette?"

Niles shakes his head and sits down next to the Mexicans, leaning forward, elbows on his knees. The padding that the mind forms around sudden and disastrous events starts to dissolve and suddenly, for the first time, he realizes what has happened. He has been ready for jail for a long time, but even so, the reality of concrete and bars and guards is stronger than he had expected. Draft evasion, Niles thinks, is an abstract name for his crime. In truth he is in jail for thinking. For thinking too clearly, for thinking too far ahead, for simply thinking at all—at the moment it doesn't matter much. What they choose to call it makes no difference. It is simply a convenient handle on his carcass, and a practical man could ask nothing more from any law.

The old man is down on the floor discovering a cigarette butt. His hands tremble so badly that he can barely negotiate the transfer from floor to mouth. He pulls himself back up onto the bench and stares at Niles. "Match?" he asks, head trembling on his thin neck, "match?" The old man asks the Mexicans and at last they understand and give him a small box of wooden matches. The old man tries to light a match but the handcuffs and his incessant trembling make it impossible. Niles takes the box of matches and strikes one and holds it out. The old man leans over to the flame but the butt is so short that he only burns his lips. Niles returns the matches to the Mexican next to him.

"What are you here for?" he asks. The Mexican shakes his head and Niles thinks for a moment. He has learned a little Spanish from one of the sprayers in the paint department. "Por qué usted está aquí?" he asks.

The Mexican shrugs. "Immigración sin pasaporte."

Niles nods and looks around the dark little holding cell. "Bienvenido á mi país."

The Mexican smiles and shakes his head and talks briefly with his friend, too quickly for Niles to follow. Niles says nothing more, and the old man searches the floor with mechanical persistence. Occasionally a guard walks by and stares into the cell. The holding cell reminds Niles of a compartment in a train and the guard a conductor, but he tries not to think where the journey is taking him.

Twenty minutes later the fat deputy unlocks the holding cell and leads Niles in to be booked. "What's the matter with the old man?" Niles asks.

"D.t.'s," the deputy says as he unlocks the door of the booking room. "Kept trying to split his head open on the bars in the drunk tank. Crazy fucker."

Niles nods. The deputy sits down at the desk in one corner of the made-over cell. Niles stands next to the desk. "Don't stand so close," the deputy says. He points with one big hand. "Over there." Niles stands for ten minutes while the deputy laboriously copies items off the arrest report onto the booking slip. He writes slowly and carefully, and after watching him for a moment Niles wants to take the pen and do it himself. The only person Niles has seen write more slowly is Boyd.

The deputy asks him questions about residence and family and occupation. When Niles names the battery factory, the deputy looks up. He has a cousin who works in that factory, in the acid department, short guy, heavy build, good boxer. Sure, Niles says, he knows him. Small world, the deputy says, and Niles agrees. Too small and getting smaller.

"Didn't want to go in the army, huh?" the deputy says. "Army isn't so bad. You can learn a trade. Lot better than doing time."

Niles says that he always thought it was about the same.

The deputy shakes his head, looking down at the forms. "Empty your pockets," he says, and points to a clear corner of the desk. "Right here."

Niles empties his pockets. He is carrying his wallet and a comb and three nickels and two small bolts and an elaborate brazing rod roach clip Lila recently made. The deputy writes each item on a receipt and puts them in a big manila envelope. When he picks up the two bolts, he asks if Niles has ever replaced the fuel pump on a Ford six. Niles says he has not. The deputy picks up the dull brass roach clip and examines it carefully, and asks "What's this for?"

Niles suspects that he already know exactly what it is for, but he figures he has nothing more to lose. Lila's tendency in roach clip design is toward the baroque. "That's the capstan rebalancer out of the tape deck in my car," Niles says, staring at it seriously.

"Oh yeah?" the deputy says. "Eight track?"

"Four," Niles tells him.

"I got an eight track," the deputy says. "Fucks up all the time." He puts the clip in the envelope and goes through Niles' wallet carefully. When he comes to Lila's high school graduation picture, he looks at it for a long moment. "Cute," he says finally, "very cute."

"Yeah," says Niles. Lila, he realizes, must think he has disappeared. "Listen," he says, "I got to make a phone call."

The deputy continues to fill out the property receipt, writing with exaggerated care.

"I have to make a phone call," Niles says, more loudly.

The deputy stops and lays his pen down and stares hard at Niles. "You think I don't got ears? Stand still and shut up. You make your phone call when I tell you to make your phone call."

"Yeah," says Niles, "right."

The deputy writes for a minute more and then has Niles sign his name in two places. He gives him the receipt and two dimes for the telephone and takes him down the hall to where a ferret-faced trustee in blue coveralls checks in his clothes and issues him a set of yellow coveralls. The coveralls are inches too large in every direction but the trustee pronounces them a good fit. He leads Niles down the corridor to a high desk where he makes three copies of fingerprints, all fingers, both hands. He presses Niles' fingers down hard, rolls them a quarter turn, and the prints come out perfectly, wide and dark. Each copy will rest in a different computerized file—one county, one state, one federal. He hands Niles a paper towel and a little bottle of special soap that washes the black ink from his fingertips easily.

In a side room next to the pay phone the trustee stands Niles against a wall, beneath darkened floodlights. With chalk he writes Niles' number on a small blackboard and he hangs the blackboard on a strap around Niles' neck. "Toes against the blue line," the trustee says, and he steps back to the camera and flashes on the floodlights. They are intensely bright and as powerful as warm sun on the face. Niles grins into the glare as broadly as he can.

The trustee stands beside the camera, his hand on a cable release. "Hey, man, make a normal face, man," he says.

Niles grins even more broadly, his face distorted with glee. "I'm happy, man, that's all."

The trustee drops the cable release and takes a step forward. "You're not happy," he says reasonably. "I've got a job to do. Don't make it hard for me."

Niles continues to grin. "I want to smile," he says through clenched teeth. "I smile for all my pictures."

"Screw you, man," the trustee says and picks up the cable release and snaps the mugshot. "Okay," he says, "all done." Niles relaxes his face and as soon as the smile is gone the trustee shoots another picture. "Screw you, smartass," the trustee repeats. "Turn sideways, toes against the red line. I don't wanna have to call a guard." Niles turns and stares at the wall.

When the pictures have been taken, the trustee leaves Niles in the corridor beside the pay phone. "Tell the guard when you're done," he says. "Take your time, man, don't hurry."

Niles finds the two dimes in the small breast pocket of the tentlike coveralls and puts one in the phone and dials the number of the apartment. It rings only once and then Lila answers.

"I think I'm fucked," Niles tells her.

Lila says she saw the car drive away, with Niles in back. "Nobody will tell me where they took you. I've been calling all over."

"County jail," Niles says, and he tells her the charges. "Call a bondsman and see what he can do. Ask around and find a lawyer. I've got about a hundred bucks saved up."

"Listen," Lila says, "there's two guys here searching the apartment. They've been going through your workbench and they're taking everything. Albert tried to stop them, but they have a warrant and I.D. and he says it's legal."

"It's okay," Niles says slowly. "Just don't let them find any dope." There are papers he should have burned, and he remembers a rough map he had made of the factory and foolishly kept in a drawer. So much for taking care, he thinks.

"The draft," Lila says. "You never told me about that."

"I forgot," Niles says. "It's not important. It's just something more to nail me with." Niles can sense Lila shaking her head at the other end of the line. He leans back against the cold concrete wall.

"We'll get you out by tonight," Lila says.

"Don't count on it," Niles says, and when there is silence, he softens it. "I mean, it's Friday. Things will be crowded."

"Albert says he'll help with bail," Lila says. "When can we come visit you?"

"I don't know," Niles says. "Just come. Bring me a book. A long one."

There is another silence. "I love you," Lila says finally, her voice much softer.

"Don't worry," Niles says, "it's going to work out."

They do not say much else, and when they hang up they both sound bad. Telephones are always difficult for Niles, but a pay phone in a county jail is nearly impossible. "Don't worry," Niles keeps saying, and it grows progressively less convincing, strained through the skein of copper cable that briefly connects them.

When he hangs up, Niles considers what to do with the other dime. He could call Carpenter, and without trying, he remembers the telephone number that was engraved on his business card. He will not call, he decides—not yet. He examines the other dime in the bright light of the jail corridor and decides that he will save it. If nothing else, it may make a good screw-driver.

The deputy in the booking room tells Niles to go sit on a bench in the hall. Niles sits and watches the traffic flow by in the corridor, prisoners and trustees and guards, each in a uniform, each on a mission, like different castes of a concrete-dwelling social insect. Friday afternoon is busy and the holding cell is full and Niles figures that a draft-evading freak is probably the safest choice to leave out in the corridor, and as time goes by and he is ignored, he begins to feel vaguely insulted.

He wanders up and down the corridor when no guards are near, but there is no place to go. Finally, about three o'clock, one of the agents who arrested Niles comes in and finds him still sitting on the bench in the corridor reading a religious magazine. He goes into the booking room and talks angrily to the fat deputy for several minutes in a voice pitched just so Niles cannot hear him. As the agent leaves, Niles says, "Whassamatter, you got to make reservations for this place?" but he walks past, saying nothing. Almost immediately, two deputies come out of the booking room and take Niles down the corridor. On a bulletin board they enter Niles' last name and number at the bottom of fifty other names under the heading CELL D—FEDERAL PRISONERS. They walk him around the end of the hall and open the second door on the left and one of them hands Niles a thin grey blanket and then he is locked into the cell.

Cell D is the size of the paint department, with two rows of metal bunk beds, ten on a side. A television is running in one corner and about twenty men are sitting on the floor, watching an afternoon game show. A woman on the show, Niles sees, has just won a television. A radio is playing loudly also, and the electronic sounds mix and collide along with the voices in the cell. Niles walks between the rows of bunks, his blanket under his arm. Most of the prisoners appear to be immigration violators, and he is almost the only Anglo on this side of the bars.

The empty bunks have no mattresses, so he climbs up on one and lies on the coil springs, using the folded blanket as a pillow. The springs dig into his back like prodding fingers. His face is three feet from the ceiling and just at the level of the unfrosted light bulb out in the corridor that shines brightly through the bars at the head of his bunk. Niles is already certain that the bulb will burn all night. He stares at the rough white ceiling, and it reminds him of the acoustical ceiling at Freeman's house, that first morning with Lila. It could be worse, Niles thinks. Somehow.

At six, three guards come down and take all the prisoners from the cell upstairs to the mess room, where they eat thick soup and stewed carrots, brown bread, coffee, and some oddly colored jello, and then they return to the cell. After the food Niles is restless, and he paces the length of the cell and talks to some prisoners. He talks to two men near his own age who were busted when their plane landed too near a retirement community out in the desert, with a hundred kilos and half a million reds aboard. Their bail is $35,-000 each, and they are annoyed because they had expected to be released for the weekend. One of them tells Niles that draft evaders have a hard time getting bail because so many of them would leave the country. Niles says he supposes that is so.

He goes back and lies on his springs and listens to the sounds of the television and radio rushing into a gentle meld of useless information over his head. A few times Lila has suggested that they leave the country. She had been reading articles in the weekly newsmagazines and she told him, "We could go to Algeria. We could live in Sweden." But Niles had always shaken his head. It was, he thought then, too soon to write off his own country, that no matter how unattractive certain of its faces might be, America was all that he could call his own, that another country would always remain an adoption—something not quite and never his home. No, he had said, he would have to stay, and he has stayed, and here he is. Official greeter, in fact: Bienvenido á mi país.

Tonight, lying in his bunk, there is no way Niles can keep himself from thinking about Lila. Albert will take good care of Lila, Niles is certain. Albert is a vulture with premonition, with perfect timing, bearing a promise of the kind of life Lila has always claimed to want. Niles knows that Lila loves him, but he does not want to deceive himself or expect more than is possible. Lila is above all practical, and if things turn out badly and Niles spends much time in jail, their next kiss could be good-bye. For a survival-oriented woman, Lila has managed to involve herself with an exceptionally disaster-bound man. He wonders briefly if Lila writes good letters. There is nothing Niles can do now: not one thing.

Except, perhaps, to escape. Staring at the ceiling, fingers locked behind his head, the idea runs in his mind like a mantra. But if he was unable to escape even on the vast outside, then there is likely not much chance for escape from the sequestered inside. But he can try; he can stay strong and alert and try, and the thought warms him like a strong brandy on a cold night in the mountains. As the eight o'clock situation comedies fill the air with bleating laughter, purpose solidifies within him as solid and firm as the trunk of an oak. He wraps the blanket around him and pillows his head on his folded coveralls and falls asleep quickly. The radio and television continue their babble until eleven o'clock and the bare light bulb in the corridor glares all night, but Niles sleeps easily and deeply. He sleeps now for a reason, and so he sleeps well.

In the morning the prisoners awaken at five-thirty for a six o'clock breakfast. Niles is stiff from sleeping on the springs and it feels good to stretch his legs on the walk up to the mess room. The breakfast is some kind of thin porridge with sugar and two slices of white toast and some stewed prunes and bad coffee. Niles sits with the three Americans from the cell—the two smugglers, and an older man busted for interstate flight with stolen credit cards. His bail is twenty thousand, and because he has a record the bondsman is making conditions and the man does not expect his wife to be able to raise it.

It is still early and so after breakfast, in the cell, half the prisoners go back to sleep while a few sweep the floor and clean the shower and toilet. Niles finds that he can sleep no longer. He lies on his bunk and once more stares at the concrete ceiling. The man in the bunk below sings himself back to sleep in a quiet perfect tenor, the Spanish words becoming gradually softer and slower and less distinct until there is just a gentle snoring.

Niles finds that in the metabolic slump of the early morning the idea of escape seems far less likely. It strikes him now as delusion, as a final romantic fantasy of the altogether-ruined, and he feels the first threads of depression enter his thinking. He decides to go talk to the smugglers again. For the sake of information he will ask them how to buy reds in quantity in Mexico. Just as he begins to climb down from his bunk, though, he hears someone calling his name. "Spindrift," the voice says, "Niles Spindrift."

"Right here," says Niles, and he walks quickly between the rows of bunks until he reaches the cell door where two deputies stand. They unlock the door and tell him he has a visitor. As they walk him up the deserted corridor, one on each side, Niles says that he didn't know the jail had visiting hours so early on Saturday morning.

"We don't," one deputy tells him.

"So how do I have a visitor?"

One guard shrugs and the other says nothing.

The long and narrow visitors' room is newly remodeled, so that the prisoner and his visitor are separated by a steel wall. Eight stools are fastened before eight thick glass windows, a black telephone receiver hanging on one side of each window and a narrow slot on the other, through which legal documents may be passed for signature. Nothing else will fit. The steel wall and the stools and the floor are all painted pale green, and with the windows, it reminds Niles of an aquarium. The deputies sit Niles on one of the center stools.

Niles looks through the window and at first sees nothing but another green wall on the other side, and then Lawrence Carpenter, beaming with early morning cheer, appears. His face swims up on the other side of the glass like a pale flat fish. Beneath thinning hair, his scalp shines in the harsh lighting.

Carpenter settles onto his high chair and adjusts his cuffs and then he picks up the telephone receiver next to him. He gestures for Niles to do the same. Niles looks over his shoulder and sees one of the guards, standing by the door, arms folded. He lifts the receiver gingerly.

"Well," Carpenter says, smiling into the telephone, his voice emerging tinny and distant from the receiver.

"You've gotten into a little trouble."

"A little," Niles says. "You got here pretty fast."

On the other side of the glass, Carpenter shrugs. "I was back east. I've been flying half the night."

"You saved me a dime," Niles says. "I was curious if

your offer of help was still good."

Carpenter smiles again, obviously pleased. "Better than ever," he says.

"You got me in here," Niles says. "Can you get me out?"

"You got yourself in here," Carpenter corrects him. "But there are still some possibilities."

"Then maybe we can do business," Niles says.

"Maybe," Carpenter says, and his smile fades. "But your bargaining position isn't very strong anymore. We're going to have to be honest with each other. That's understood."

"Of course," Niles says.

"We know quite a bit about what you've been doing the last few months," Carpenter tells him. "Enough to be very curious."

"I've been doing some pretty curious things," Niles says.

"You should know one thing," Carpenter says, unblinking. "We have the device."

Niles stares through the thick glass and says nothing. It had to happen, he knew that, but he did not expect it so quickly.

"That's not a bluff. Thirty men searched the factory all night," Carpenter says. "That's triple-time for county sheriffs. It took us all night, and at that we were lucky." Carpenter pauses for a moment, licks his lips. "I think you've built something remarkable, Niles, but planting it in the factory was not a bright thing to do. Monday morning an additional charge of sabotage of defense production will be filed against you in district court."

Niles nods slowly. They have the device and his notes and that is all they need. His bargaining position is, indeed, weak.

"We have your notes and schematics, of course," Carpenter says. "But they're rather cryptic."

"They're perfectly clear," Niles says, looking down at the slick black plastic of the telephone, wondering how many more times he will be speaking into it.

"Well," Carpenter shrugs. "We'd like you to explain a few things to us. Listen to this, Niles: in the eyes of the government, that kind of cooperation would take precedence over present or future legal action against you stemming from this arrest."

Niles looks at him. At least Carpenter is honest about the nature of his snare. When your snare is good enough, Niles figures, you can afford to be honest. It is his only chance. "All right," he says, and then that sounds too easy. "Can I keep the patents in my own name?"

"Of course," Carpenter says. "Innovators deserve their reward. You're going to be very wealthy, very famous."

"All right," Niles says. "Then get me out of here. Today, if you can."

Carpenter's smile resumes, as if a cloud has passed from before the August sun, and he looks ready to thrust his forearm through the glass and shake hands to seal the bargain. "I think," he says, "and in fact I am almost certain, that it can be very easily done."

Carpenter hangs up his receiver, and after a moment Niles replaces his in its chrome cradle, and the two guards escort him back to his cell. Neither touches him, he notices, and in fact he senses a certain respect in their manners. In the cell, he feels briefly ill—he thinks it may be from the breakfast—but it passes, and then, he feels nothing at all.

In less than two hours, Niles and Carpenter are sitting in the back seat of a pale-grey official car, driving toward the center of town, surrounded by the bright morning glare of Santa Teresa. Santa Teresa is a sweaty, sprawling town, dusted by the airborne pollutants of the L.A. Basin, chopped into random-shaped segments by six- or eight-lane freeways, with a downtown of all-day theaters and credit jewelry stores that collapse and are abandoned as they reach the terminal stages of urban molder. Carpenter removes Niles' handcuffs and gives them to the silent driver, and Niles concludes from the shape of the driver's jacket that he is armed.

"I'm sorry all of this had to happen," Carpenter says, leaning back and putting one thick arm up on the seat behind Niles. "It must have been very unpleasant."

Niles shrugs, rubbing his wrists from the grip of the handcuffs. "It was an education."

"That's the best way to look at it," Carpenter says. "What's done is done." He is silent for a moment, looking at Niles, his eyes clear behind the spotless lenses of his eyeglasses. "You've been released under my recognizance," he says. "That's a large responsibility for me. I hope you'll keep that in mind."

"I appreciate it," Niles says. "It's a great favor."

"Don't mention it," Carpenter says. "It's only the beginning. We have some big plans for you. I hope you're ready to travel. New York and then Washington, how does that sound?"

It sounds supremely miserable to Niles. If there are any two places in the world he does not need to go to, they are New York and Washington. He stares at his steel-creased wrists. "Well," he says finally, "I might need a few days to get ready. Straighten out my thinking a bit."

Carpenter purses his lips, considers this. "You have doubts?" he asks. "Hesitations?"

Niles watches the driver, who, machinelike, concentrates on his driving. A bit of toilet paper on his cheek marks a hurried Sunday shave. "Frankly," Niles tells Carpenter, "I don't trust you."

Carpenter shakes his head, as if he has heard this too often. "Before we go any further, Niles," he says patiently, "let's get one thing straight. I want you to understand that we recognize in your work unlimited prospects for the benefit of all mankind."

"I'd like to believe that," Niles says agreeably. "It would make things a lot easier for both of us."

"Let me give you one example that just occurred to me this morning while I was shaving. With proper modifications, I think your device could be a powerful weapon in our fight against mental illness. Do you believe me when I say that?"

"Sure," Niles says, "I believe you."

"Niles, I don't think you know just how far we've thought this thing through in terms of its applications for better living. Consider your device, with minor changes, used as an escapant. As mental recreation, as an alternative to the dangerous chemicals that are destroying your generation. Think of the constructive lives we could save that way. These are the interests of your people I'm talking about, Niles, not the interests of some imaginary emperor warlords."

Both Albert and Carpenter, Niles thinks, have great facility for gluing totally opposite interests back-to-back and peddling them as the same thing. It is not so much a talent, he decides, as simply malfunctioning perception. "Could be," he tells Carpenter.

"Do I begin to make my point?" Carpenter asks. "Can I make you see that you are trying to escape your destined social role? That to withhold the benefits of your work from other human beings is irresponsible and immature and entirely selfish?"

"You could be right," Niles says. "You could easily be right." If he begins to disagree with Carpenter this soon, he knows, he will be back in the handcuffs before he has a chance to scratch his nose. He looks out the window and sees that they are nearing the center of town.

"We're going to sign some papers at the courthouse," Carpenter says. "Just some formalities."

"Can that wait?" Niles asks. "I'd like to go see my old lady first. You're invited for dinner."

"Next stop," Carpenter says. He smiles. "I don't think you know how hard it is to get hippies out of jail on Saturday in this county. Just be patient."

Niles is not patient at all. He needs to talk to Lila, to make plans, to decide where he stands. "Okay," he says, and settles back in the seat, arms folded.

"I hear Lila is a beautiful girl," Carpenter says.

"She's all right," Niles says.

Carpenter nods. "She's included in all this, of course," he says. "Pretty soon you'll be able to treat her like a queen."

"She'll love that," Niles says.

"And it's only going to get better," Carpenter says. "You're on your way."

They ride in silence for a minute or so. "How did

you find me?" Niles asks finally. "I've been pretty careful."

Carpenter shakes his head. "You'll be flattered. There was a five thousand dollar reward on you. We just got word yesterday that you were here."

"From who?"

Carpenter shrugs, looks out the window. "Does it matter? It's all over now."

"It matters," Niles says. "I'm curious. I deserve to know my own story. Was it someone in Morton?"

"Well," Carpenter says, "I don't see that it's necessary—"

"I want to know," Niles says. "Didn't we agree to be honest with each other?"

Carpenter thinks about this for a moment and then nods. He looks at Niles. "It was Lila's friend Albert. I think he was staying with you. He's been looking for you for some time."

Niles stares at the back of the driver's neck, thick and pale and close-shaven. The idea makes instant and perfect sense. He has seriously underestimated Albert in every respect, and Niles hopes now that he will have a chance to discuss all of this with him, at length.

"I don't want you to hold this against him," Carpenter says. "He's a bright young man. I think we'll be employing him on a permanent basis."

"Maybe you better keep him away from me for a while," Niles says. "Let me get used to the idea."

Carpenter shakes his head. "Someday you'll thank Albert for what he's done—the world will thank him. We're going to form a long and profitable association."

Niles nods slowly. Not if he can help it.

Carpenter leans over and unlocks a heavy leather briefcase on the car floor. He reaches inside and brings out a thick cloth bag closed by a drawstring. "Look at it this way," he says to Niles, and he opens the bag and takes out the small silver chassis of the mindfogger and holds it in his hand. "We share a tool of great importance, and we're going to have to cooperate with each other. Agreed?"

Niles looks at the mindfogger. He has not seen it for weeks and now it appears tiny and harmless and unimportant. Only the red microswitch breaks the smooth shiny expanse of the metal box.

Carpenter sees the expression on Niles' face and smiles. "You probably think I'm stupid," he says, "to have this where you can reach over and switch it on."

"You're no fool," Niles says. "You've removed the batteries."

Carpenter shakes his head. "We didn't have to," he says. "It's broken." He punches the microswitch several times and hands the little box to Niles. "Completely defective."

Niles turns the box over in his hands. Now he notices that one corner of the aluminum case has been badly dented. "What did you do to it?" he asks.

"We've been trying to repair it," Carpenter says. "The man who found it fell off a urinal and the box hit the floor and stopped working. Since then we've tried everything we could. The circuit seems to be intact. It just won't work."

Niles shakes his head. He is puzzled. "There's not that much that can go wrong with it," he says slowly.

"Those coils," Carpenter says. "The ones on the ferrite forms. No one in the lab had seen anything like those before. They appear to be totally useless."

Niles shrugs. "There are some ideas I'll have to explain to you," he says. "It may take awhile. I've never tried to say them out loud before." He opens the aluminum case and looks inside. The circuit boards and wiring harnesses appear to be undamaged. He sticks his tongue across the battery terminals and tastes the coppery sting of charge. The circuit should be working. He puts the box back together and gazes for a moment out the window, trying to think what might be wrong.

They are in the middle of town now, probably not far from the courthouse, driving very fast through the busy Saturday traffic. The car is just approaching an intersection where the light is green. Niles looks down at the mindfogger, still puzzled, and idly presses the small red switch and then it occurs to him that the car is going too fast to stop for the yellow light that has just appeared at the intersection ahead and that some-one should do something about it but the driver doesn't appear to notice and the car is just drifting toward the intersection where the light is now red and the traffic is starting across right in front of them and they are still traveling at thirty-five miles an hour cruising into the intersection and then there is a blare of horns that sud-denly dies into a sound like empty trash cans being thrown out of a high window onto concrete and then an incredible concussion and the rubbery scream of tires and the four corners of the intersection spinning past the windows like a carnival ride and then nothing.

When Niles opens his eyes he knows they have been closed for only a moment. His right shoulder aches sharply where he was thrown against the back of the front seat, and as he tries to sit up he struggles to think what is happening. The windshield in front of the driver is wildly starred and the driver slumps sideways, one arm twisted in the plastic spokes of the steering wheel. Carpenter has gone over the front seat entirely and is crumpled against the dashboard, head toward the floor, his shoulders moving with slow unconscious breathing. Niles feels blackness rising up in his eyes and he looks down and sees the mindfogger on the car floor and punches the switch again and immediately his mind clears.

The pain in his shoulder is sharp but not serious. He

must think clearly. He tries to open the door on his side but it is buckled too severely. He slides over to the other side where the door is sprung partially open, the window smashed, and he kicks it the rest of the way and stumbles out onto the glass-strewn pavement.

Standing in the sunlight, dizziness again overtakes him and he leans against the car for a moment and looks across the intersection. They have hit a truck, and picked up two more cars in their crazy spin across the intersection. From all directions people are beginning to converge on the accident. Traffic has stopped and the sidewalks are lining with gawkers. Someone, a girl in a nurse's uniform, steps toward him. Niles reaches back into the car and gets the mindfogger and then he starts to run as hard as he can.

His head is still light and he feels as if his feet are barely touching the pavement but he keeps his balance, and with the small case in one hand he pushes through the crowds of people and sprints up the street, until he sees an open alley off to the left. He turns and as he enters the alley he hears the sirens start, somewhere close to the accident. He runs without thinking, using narrow alleys and empty side streets to take himself as far from the intersection as possible, running until he can feel his heart pounding in his head like delicate hammers on the eardrums, louder now than the diminishing sirens. He runs in the direction of the high mountains to the northeast, and after a mile or so the city starts to thin out and there are occasional vacant lots and a large park with a few palm trees and then finally an orange grove.

Niles runs crouching between the dense orange trees until he is concealed from the road. He falls to his knees, and then sits at the edge of a shallow irrigation ditch and places the mindfogger on the packed dirt beside him. For a moment he works to quiet his breathing, and then listens carefully. He is certain that no one has followed him from the accident.

His curiosity overcomes his exhaustion. There is something he does not understand. He picks up the mindfogger and presses the switch and once more the warm buzzing spreads through his head. He shuts it off, quickly this time. It appears to work normally. He praises his luck, and then the delayed shock of the accident sets in and his hands tremble, his stomach rises like a balloon, and he leans back against the tree and closes his eyes. There will be time to think about the mindfogger, about everything, later.

Niles spends the afternoon in the orange grove. The trees are old and need to be cut back and they offer him good cover. No one comes through this portion of the grove and Niles relaxes, leaning against the tree, legs stretched out to the edge of the water-filled ditch. His head remains light and his shoulder continues to ache, but once the shock subsides he decides that it could not be serious. Things could be much worse, he thinks: now at least he has a chance, perhaps a good chance, to stay free a little longer. The image of the mountains as he fled the accident, looming up like a grey-purple wall above the valley, continues to fill his head, even though within the confines of the grove he can no longer see them. He had run toward the mountains out of unreasoned instinct, the unfiltered reaction of flight, and now the idea of them is a persistent vision.

The patches of light that filter through the orange trees shift gradually around his feet as the horizon lifts to meet the sun. By dusk he is hungry, and he walks through the heart of the grove searching for fruit ripe enough to eat. He consumes a few hard sour oranges as the stars appear amid the thick foliage of the trees, and when he has finished, it is dark. Niles knows that the waning moon will not rise until early in the morning, but even so, he will have to be careful—by now, he is certain, every cop in the county will be looking for him.

In the darkness, he leaves the trees and heads for Morton and Lila. It is a distance of seven or eight miles, and he tries to cover it quickly, taking unlighted dirt side roads and staying close to the groves. On the long straight roads he sees headlights at a great distance and has time to move far back into the trees. He walks the dark roads in long strides, mindfogger in one hand, thick masses of trees on either side, the black sky starry above his head, the soft grating of his boots on the gravel roadbeds the only sound in the warm still air. Soon, when his eyes have grown accustomed to the dim starlight, Niles feels like a part of the night, natural and at ease, and the air enfolds him, just the temperature of flesh. He sights on Mars, now rising low and bright red in the southeast, and follows it home like a beacon.

It is past midnight when Niles reaches the outskirts of Morton. He comes out of the trees and crosses two roads and begins to walk at the unlighted edges of the big packinghouse yards, alert for night watchmen and guard dogs, until he draws close to the half-darkened streets of downtown.

He halts at the edge of a warehouse just before town and stands for several minutes, watching the deserted streets, the half-lit store windows. The closer he is to home the more he is pulled to hurry, and the more he forces himself to be cautious. At last he crosses the empty main highway and goes into a long dark alley, lined with discarded cardboard cartons and trash bins. He follows it through the heart of downtown, dashing across the wide side streets, and finally he emerges facing the big white stucco YMCA. He cuts across the grass field behind the Y until he reaches the first row of houses, and then he starts climbing fences.

He approaches Delores' by way of backyards in order to avoid the streets. He buttons the mindfogger inside his shirt so that both hands are free and as he goes over the high fences he tries to be as quiet as possible. The strain of lifting over the fences tears at his bad shoulder and he favors the other. He goes past clotheslines and children's swings and playhouses and doghouses and rosebushes, all vague outlines in the dim lights of the stars and the street lamps out by the sidewalks. He moves without thinking, allowing the rhythm of his movements to take over and carry him from step to step without hesitation. He is lucky, and moves almost silently, and only once does he hear a dog growl from within a screened porch, but the growl fades even before he is gone.

In fifteen minutes he drops down from the top of a grapestake fence into the darkest and most distant corner of Delores' backyard. He sees lights upstairs, and uses the heel of his boot to dig a hole in the loose dry dirt at his feet, close to the fence. When the hole is six inches deep and as many across, he unbuttons his shirt and takes out the mindfogger and buries it, setting it in the hole on its side so that the pressure of the topsoil will not activate the switch. He packs the soil down with his boot and smooths the surface with a dry branch and then he is ready.

Niles goes up the wooden stairs that ascend to Delores' back door two at a time, putting his weight down slowly so that the old warped wood creaks slowly and almost inaudibly. At the top he stands on the landing and looks in through the screened window. He sees the empty hallway and, through the living room door, the back of Delores' overstuffed sofa. Albert and Lila are sitting on the sofa, talking.

Lila sits a short distance from Albert, who is speaking to her in a low voice, gesturing with one hand, his other arm up on the back of the sofa. Niles makes no sound moving into the darkened hallway. He crosses the hall and stands silently at the door to the living room, fifteen feet from Albert and Lila. The first step Niles takes into the living room makes Albert look over his shoulder.

"What—" Albert says as he sees Niles, and then he is up off the sofa and stepping toward the front window that looks down on the street. Lila turns and sees Niles and her mouth opens. Albert rushes for the window and Niles goes over the end of the sofa and tackles him around the knees and brings him down, Albert's head just missing the window frame. Albert rolls over onto his back and starts to get up but Niles rises to one knee and throws a hard right to the side of Albert's jaw and feels the bone move beneath his fist. Albert grunts, falls back, one hand in front of his face, and Niles pins him to the floor, knees dug into his shoulders. Albert struggles to rise for a moment and then he opens his mouth and Niles whips the back of his knuckles across his face. Albert's head rolls, and he opens his mouth again and Niles closes it again with the back of his knuckles, much harder, taking a long swing, snapping his wrist, hearing Albert's head bounce on the hardwood floor, and this time Albert is still. Blood runs from the corner of his mouth and his nose, and his eyes are closed. Niles feels sudden fury at Albert's inertness, but he shakes his head and relaxes his hands. His shoulder now throbs sharply, insistently.

He wipes his fists on Albert's slacks and slowly stands. He moves next to the front window and looks out carefully. Down on the street, between two streetlights, is a sheriff's patrol car, the shadowy figures of two men sitting in the front seat.

Lila is standing now, staring at Albert unconscious on the floor, and Niles goes back around the sofa and takes her in his arms. Her hair is tied back and she smells of bath soap. She holds him tightly, saying nothing. "It's okay," he says softly into her ear. "It's okay."

Delores, awakened by the sound of Niles and Albert hitting the floor, comes into the living room, wrapped in her rhinestone-buttoned bathrobe, her feet in woolly slippers, her curly hair disarrayed, her face pale and sleepy. In one glance she takes in the living room scene.

"Oh my God," Delores says. "Oh my dear God."

Niles looks over Lila's shoulder at Delores. Her mouth half-open, she appears about to scream. "It's all right," he tells her. "Sit down, I'll explain."

Delores shakes her head, glancing at Niles for only a moment. She goes over to Albert and kneels beside him and picks up his head and wipes his face with the quilted sleeve of her robe.

"They told us you were in an accident," Lila says to Niles. "There were cops here in the afternoon, but they left."

Niles nods. "They're still on the street."

"Albert is working for them, isn't he?"

Niles nods again. Lila holds him even tighter, her body warm against his. "I'm so glad," she says, "I'm so glad you're here. Albert was talking to me about his ranch. He said you wouldn't come back."

Behind them Albert groans, very quietly. "You broke his teeth," Delores says. "You broke his teeth."

"We have to take care of Albert," Niles says. "I'll tell you more later. Go get the nylon line and the hunting knife out of my pack."

Lila lets Niles go, reluctantly, and goes into the bedroom. Niles crouches next to Delores on the floor. "Why did you do this?" Delores asks as she pillows Albert's head on a cushion from the sofa. As she speaks she does not look at Niles. "I think you're crazy. He never did anything to you."

"He did enough," Niles says, rubbing the new pain in his shoulder. "He put me in jail."

Delores looks at him. "No," she says, "he couldn't have."

Niles shrugs. "Keep his head up. Don't let him swallow any teeth."

"This is crazy," Delores says, to no one in particular, as a public declaration. "You can't go around hitting people."

Lila returns with the coil of rope and Niles' long knife, and sets them on the floor. Delores sees them and her eyes widen. "What are you going to do with those? What are you going to do to Albert?"

Niles hears the first shrill note of hysteria in her voice. "Why don't you two go in the kitchen?" Niles says quietly to Lila and Delores. "I'll be done here in a minute."

Lila holds one of Delores' arms and tries to make her rise.

"No," says Delores, "this is my apartment. I want to stay here."

"Come on," Lila says softly, "it's all right. Come on."

Niles decides there has been enough discussion. "Get out of here," he says. "Both of you."

Delores rises slowly, shaking her head, and follows Lila to the kitchen. "I don't understand," she is saying to Lila. "What the hell does he think he's doing?"

Albert remains just at the edge of consciousness. Niles checks to see that his mouth is not bleeding badly and then rolls him over on his stomach. He puts Albert's hands together, wrist to wrist, and lashes them securely with the nylon line. He crosses Albert's ankles and ties them also and then runs a double length of line between wrists and ankles and pulls it up until Albert's knees are bent, his feet close to his hands. The knots are firm and the lines tight and Niles knows that Albert will go nowhere.

Albert's body tenses as Niles rolls him onto his side. "What are you doing?" Albert asks, working his swelling jaw with difficulty. His eyes are wide and he is clearly frightened. "What are you doing to me?"

Niles looks into his face. "I tied you up. You'll have to stay tied for a while. I'll leave the TV on."

"My mouth," Albert mumbles, "you wrecked my mouth."

Niles holds Albert's jaw and moves it gently from side to side. Albert jerks his head away. "That hurts," he says.

"Isn't broken," Niles says. "You'd know if it was broken. You'll be fine." He taps the handle of his knife on the floor. "More than you deserve."

"I was trying to help you," Albert says, slowly, with effort. "I wanted to get you the best deal possible." He closes his eyes, opens them again. "Partners, man, we were going to be partners."

Niles shakes his head. "You and I could never be partners."

Niles leaves Albert on the floor where he first fell and starts into the kitchen. He switches off the living room light, for the benefit of the cops on the street, and then he turns back to Albert. "Listen, you don't make any noise, I don't have to gag you, okay? I never gagged anyone before. I might be kind of clumsy."

Albert nods, curled on the floor, and Niles goes into the kitchen. Lila and Delores are both seated at the table and Delores' face is drained as pale white as its enamel surface. She has caught glimpses of what was happening through the kitchen door. "He's hurt and you've got him tied up like a pig," she tells Niles. "What do you want?"

Niles says nothing. He finds some bread and cheese

and sits at the table. Lila brings him milk and offers to heat soup but Niles says, "No time." As he eats he explains about Albert. Delores says she doesn't believe it.

"I think it's true," Lila tells Delores.

"Believe me," Niles says.

Delores stares at him. This intrusion of violence into her life has left her without bearings. "I don't know," she says. "I just don't want anybody to get hurt."

"Albert won't get hurt," Niles says. "He's not really hurt now. Nobody is going to get hurt."

Delores shakes her head and is silent. Niles tells her to go out and watch Albert and keep him quiet. "Tell him that I threatened you with a knife," Niles says, setting his knife in the center of the table. The worn black leather sheath shines dully in the kitchen light. "Say that you're frightened. Then you won't be an accessory. Trust me, just for a while."

Delores hesitates for a moment, looks at Lila, who nods, and then she says: "All right. For a while."

She begins to leave and Niles holds her forearm, hard, for a moment. "Delores, don't untie him, I mean it."

Delores nods and Niles lets her arm go and she walks out of the kitchen. For a moment there is silence.

"You can't stay here," Lila tells him finally. "They'll be back tomorrow. They think you're hurt, laid up outside of town."

Niles nods as he swallows the last of his food. "I know," he says, "I need to hide." He lowers his voice so that it cannot be heard in the living room. "Listen," he says, "do you think I could hide in the mountains? Somewhere way off the trails? Just for a couple of weeks."

Lila looks uncertain. "I don't know," she says. "Around here, it'll be hard. There's no real wilderness left."

"But if I was careful, if I kept far away from people? Just until the search dies down."

Lila shrugs. "You can try," she says. "You might be safer than if you stayed down here and tried to travel."

Niles nods. "I've been thinking about it all day. There's not much else I can do."

Lila stares at the top of the table. "I'll come too," she says at last.

Niles looks up. "You want to?" He had expected that she would stay in Morton, that they would meet and travel when it was safer.

Lila nods. From the living room Delores' voice is a low murmur. "I'll come," Lila says, and then she adds quickly: "Unless you don't want me to."

Niles is silent for a moment, weighing the idea. He wants her with him. "I don't know what will happen," he says.

"That's all right," Lila says. "Somebody's got to look after you."

Niles looks at her closely. "Yeah?"

Lila shrugs and tries to smile. "What else is there to do in a town like this?"

"Okay," Niles says slowly. "Okay. I can't promise anything except that we won't get bored."

"That's good enough," she says.

Niles brings his pack from the closet. Lila left her pack and sleeping bag in Los Angeles, so they put everything in Niles': a few pounds of rice, a few pounds of oats, a can of shortening, flour, some sugar, some salt, packages of dried soup, a sack of dried fruit. There is nothing else in Delores' cupboards worth carrying. Niles packs his fishing rod and leader and a box of flies. He has an old goosedown sleeping bag, and he rolls that up with two woollen blankets and begins to tie it on the outside of the pack when Lila stops him.

"Hold it," she says, "you think you're going to carry all that stuff?"

"Well," he says. He lifts the pack. The mass of it already pulls at his bad shoulder and he grimaces at the thought of the walking to come.

"You'll fall on your face," Lila says. She takes the sleeping bag and the blankets and ties them into a bundle with a length of line from the pack, with loops she can slip over her shoulders, padded with two folded washcloths.

Niles goes out into the dark living room and gets the rest of the nylon line. Delores is sitting on the floor next to Albert, faintly illuminated by the square patch of light falling from the kitchen door. Albert watches Niles carefully.

"So what are you going to do now?" Delores asks him as he coils the line on one arm.

Niles shrugs, looks at Albert, then looks back at the line. "Not much I can do," he says. "I don't know."

Albert, curled on the floor like a comma, stares, saying nothing.

"You should give yourself up," Delores says. "I really think you're only making things worse."

"No," Niles says. "Things can't get much worse."

He goes back in the kitchen. Lila has put some cooking utensils in the pack and now it leans, bulging, obviously heavy, against one kitchen cabinet. She has unrolled the blankets and sleeping bag so that she can put spare clothes inside, along with some candles and soap and bandages and her birth control pills. Niles grins when he sees the pills, and he tugs at Lila's hair.

Niles goes into the bedroom and stops at his workbench. All of his old notebooks and most of his tools are gone, the metal drawers have been pulled out and left on the floor, only a few stray, bent components remain scattered across the top of the bench. He picks up a blank notebook and a pen from beneath his chair to carry in the pack, and then, just before he turns away, he notices the electromagnetic spectrum poster. It has been torn down and now lies, crumpled, on the floor behind the bench. He picks it up, folds it carefully, slips it into the notebook.

It is four o'clock, and Niles knows the sun will begin to rise in another hour. While Lila is lacing her boots he carries the heavy pack out into the hall and leaves it leaning next to the back door.

In the living room, Niles tells Delores to get dressed. She looks up from Albert, her rhinestone buttons sparkling in the light from the kitchen. "Why?"

"I want you to help us."

Delores is silent for a moment and then Albert says quietly, "Go ahead. He's not going to get far."

Delores goes to dress and Niles sends Lila down the back stairs to warm up the car. The old Ford stalls when cold, and Niles knows they can't afford to waste any time. Soon he can hear the car, running quietly, in the driveway behind the house. Niles goes to the front window and pulls the shade back slightly and looks out onto the street. The sheriff's car has not moved. "Shit," he says softly.

Albert has been watching carefully. "You don't have a chance," he says. "You can't even get out of the driveway."

Niles stares at Albert on the floor, without seeing him. There is only one chance, and even that is very slight. Delores comes out of her room, wearing slacks and a light jacket. She stands in the hall, waiting.

Niles rehearses what he will say and then goes to the telephone in the kitchen. As he dials the number of the police department he covers the mouthpiece with a thin dish towel. A female voice answers, and Niles coughs, once, twice, and then speaks with a high breathless elderly quaver. There is a young man with long hair in his backyard, he tells the woman. He was trying to climb over the fence from the next yard and he slipped and fell onto the patio and isn't moving now. Niles says he has all the doors locked and the young man is just lying there. Niles gives her an address, two blocks down from Delores' and one across, somewhere between the duplex and the YMCA. The woman repeats the address and says someone will be right out. Niles says thank you with elaborate dignity and hangs up. His hands are shaking, and Delores is staring at him, frowning, puzzled.

Niles goes into the living room and steps over Albert and pulls the shade aside again. The sheriff's car sits gleaming in the incandescence of the streetlights. After ten seconds or so, Niles can hear the engine fire, rev a few times, the headlights flick on, and the car does an abrupt U-turn in front of the duplex and heads down the street. Through the window the screech of tires, the scream of acceleration, are soft and muted.

"Let's go," Niles says to Delores, and moves past her in the hallway and throws the bulky pack onto his good shoulder. He sees Delores hesitate at the doorway to the living room. "He'll be all right," Niles says. "You'll be back in an hour." He holds Delores' arm and pushes her down the wooden stairs in front of him. He puts Delores and the pack in the back seat and then runs to the corner of the yard and uncovers the mindfogger.

Lila has moved aside in the front seat, and Niles slides in behind the wheel. He hands the mindfogger to Lila and slips the car into reverse and then they are out of the driveway, onto the street, turning in the opposite direction from the sheriff's car. Niles stays on the side streets, leaves town as quickly as possible, and heads through the groves toward the foothills of the Santa Teresa mountains. The car is filled with the green glow of the dashlights, and in the still calm air of the early morning there is already the faintest hint of sunrise.

Niles watches the rear-view mirror, Lila sits straight-backed, glancing over her shoulder, and Delores stretches out in the back seat, leaning against the pack. The car speeds between the trees, a cocoon of spun silence, and when the long straight road behind them has been empty for some time and the mass of the mountains looms before them, Lila nods her head.

"I think we made it," she says to Niles. "I think we're safe."

"We won't be safe for a long time," Niles says. "Not for a long time."

In an hour they have climbed seven thousand feet. The sky is growing yellow-pink in the east as the old Ford moves through hills covered with pine and mesquite. Niles drives fast, and on the sharper curves the front wheels shimmy and Delores swears softly in the back seat.

"Hey," Delores says finally, "tell me, what's this going to get you?"

"A few weeks," Niles says, eyes on the road. "Some time."

Delores shakes her head. "This is your big fantasy," she says to Lila, "isn't it? Running away to the mountains."

Lila shrugs. "It's no fantasy," she says.

"They'll get you in the mountains," Delores says quietly, "don't you know that?"

"They'll have to find us first," Lila says.

"You think that's going to be hard?"

Lila is silent. Niles shrugs, and notices in the movement that his right shoulder has begun to stiffen up. "It could be," he says, and then he pauses to choose his words. "People are going to be asking you where we went," he says. "Probably a lot of people. No matter what they say, tell them you don't know. Tell them you took us to Los Angeles and you heard one of us talk about Canada but you don't really know. Be consistent, and they won't bother you again."

"All right," Delores says, after a moment. "I'll try. But I don't know if it will make much difference."

"Try hard," Lila says. "Don't tell anyone. Don't tell Albert."

"Okay," Delores says. "I already said I wouldn't. But if I did, it would only be to help."

"We won't need help," Niles says. "Don't say anything."

The sky brightens and the stars fade and the air grows cooler as the car rises above the valley. Finally Lila sets the heater on. "It's good we brought the blankets," she says.

In the faint blue light Delores is examining the terrain. "This sounds like a bad idea to me," she offers from the back seat. "This is the real woods. You could get hurt. Then what would you do?"

"Don't worry," Niles says. "We'll take care of each other."

The angle of the road grows steeper, and the car slows as it beings to climb a set of short switchbacks. Finally the road enters a small flat valley containing a low stream and a sparse forest of scrub pine. The stream is the western boundary of a wilderness area. Above the stream the mountain slopes are dark and thick with pines, broken only by rocky ravines and the barren expanses of granite that tower above tree line.

The sun is edging over the horizon just as Niles pulls the car off onto the narrow gravel shoulder of the road. This early, the two-lane highway is deserted as far as Niles can see in both directions. He leans forward in the front seat, staring at the formations above them, orienting himself to the shape of the land. Once, when planning a weekend hiking trip that never materialized, Lila had bought topographic maps of this area. The two maps are now folded near the front of the pack.

"There's a ranger station up the road," Niles says. "I want to stay away from that."

Lila is looking around. "We should get up into the trees before it gets any lighter."

"Jesus," Delores says, "there's no trail here, no nothing."

"This is fine," Niles says, and he gets out of the car into the cool morning air. Lila follows, carrying the bedroll, and Niles pulls the pack out of the back seat, leaning it up against a low pine growing close to the road. Delores climbs out after the pack.

For a moment the three stand in silence, Delores by the car, Niles and Lila beside the bulky pack and bedroll. Already the sun is higher, the sky a deepening blue, the night chill dissolving in the sharply angled yellow sunlight. "Well," Delores says finally, "I guess I'd better get back." With one hand she smooths down her curly hair, still tangled from her abrupt awakening, but she does not move. "I guess there's nothing else you need now, is there?"

Niles shakes his head. "I think we're on our own."

"Here," Delores says, and she holds out a handful of bills, twenty-five dollars or so, the paper palely green against the deeper color of the trees. "Take this. It's all I have right now."

Lila takes the money and puts her arms around Delores. "Be careful," Delores says softly. "Good luck."

"Don't tell anyone where we've gone," Lila repeats. "No matter who."

"All right," Delores says, and she holds Lila for another moment. Then she turns to Niles.

"Thanks," he says. "Thanks for everything."

She nods and looks at him for a long time, searching his face. "I hope you know what you're doing," she tells him, "take care of yourselves," and then she turns away and starts to walk back around the car. "So long," she says as she opens the door and gets behind the wheel.

Lila waves and the car starts up, the first blast of

blue exhaust scatters a few dry pine needles and the brake lights flash jewel-red for a moment. Delores locks the wheels and the car slowly creaks through a U-turn, driving onto the other shoulder of the narrow road, then straightening out, aiming down the highway, gathering speed, growing smaller, disappearing at last among the thick low pines that crowd up close to the asphalt. Niles and Lila stand at the edge of the deserted highway and listen to the sound of the Ford far down the road, past their vision, until a slight breeze rises from down the slope, and then there is nothing but the brushing of the morning air in the tops of the trees.

In twenty mintues Niles knows that it will not be so easy. They have climbed half a mile from the road, pushing through the dry scrubby patches of manzanita and the short twisted pines, until at last they reach the level of a well-worn trail that winds up to the spine of the range. They have climbed fast in order to get out of sight of the road, and both Niles and Lila are breathing hard. Niles' shoulder has begun to throb with each step, and when they are shielded by the trees, Lila helps him slide the heavy pack off his shoulders and they lean it against a boulder of fine-grained granite. Lila sets the bedroll beside it.

Niles sits on a smaller rock, beneath a high pine, and tries to rub away the dull ache that has centered itself deep in his shoulder. Already he feels tired, and his head seems to be growing light from lack of sleep.

Lila, still standing, the sleeves of her old wool shirt rolled past her elbows, rocks the pack back and forth. "I'm not too tired," she says. "I could take the pack for a while."

Niles shakes his head. "I'll get used to it."

"I could carry some more stuff in the blankets," she says.

"It's okay," Niles says, "don't worry."

"You're sure?" Lila asks. "You look pale."

"Don't worry," Niles repeats. He leans forward, elbows on his knees. Through the trees, he can see the empty ribbon of road below them, and far beyond that, the brown haze of the immense valley to the west.

Lila lifts the pack. She raises it a foot off the ground, lowers it again quickly. She shakes her head. "How far are we going?"

"Fifteen miles, maybe," Niles says, without moving. "Ten on the trail, five off." By nightfall he wants to cross the high rocky pass two thousand feet above them, over to the other side of the range, into one of the long isolated valleys that stretch down onto the high desert floor. On that side, as the valleys drop onto the desert, they grow dry and fill with mesquite and rattlesnakes, but near the top the streams run all summer and there are tall stands of pine.

"Well," Lila says, "we'll go slow."

"Most likely," Niles says. "But not too slow."

The first five miles of the trail climb steadily, gaining fifteen hundred feet of elevation, through increasing vegetation. On one side a stream parallels the trail, rushing glasslike over the rocks, surrounded by pines and willows, its banks spattered with bright green summer growth and small yellow wildflowers. The water tastes cold and sweet. On the other side a dry slope bears mesquite and darker manzanita, the manzanita still dotted with the dusty pink blooms of the spring.

Finally, when the sun has reached its highest point in the sky, Lila says that she wants to stop. Niles nods: even the slightest movement of the pack now sends long runners of pain down the bones of his arm. His head aches as well and he is beginning to take careless steps. He is ready to rest. "A little food," Lila tells him, "and we'll walk twice as fast."

They leave the trail and walk down to a small

shaded clearing. Lila sees the face Niles makes as he takes his pack off.

"Sit down and rest," she says. "I can take care of this."

"No," Niles says, "it's all right," but he sits anyway, leaning back against a rotting log.

There is little in the pack to eat cold, so Lila gathers wood and builds a small fire, balancing a pot on two rocks to boil water for rice. Niles watches for a few minutes and then he rises and walks carefully down to the stream, to a flat marshy area that is just beginning to dry in the heat of the California summer and, at the edge of the shady dampness, he picks handfuls of a light green wild lettuce. He carries the wide leaves back to the fire, and Lila cuts them into strips and boils them with the rice.

The combination tastes very good, but when Niles tries to eat with his right hand, he discovers that the fingers have grown faintly numb.

Lila sees his difficulty. "Your arm's worse, isn't it?" she asks, when they have finished eating.

Niles begins to shrug, but thinks better of it.

"Did you look at it?" Lila asks.

"No."

"Well," she says, "you should look at it." She unbuttons his shirt and he leans forward, sliding it first off his left shoulder, then, gingerly, his right.

"Jesus," Lila says softly, "Jesus Christ."

Niles looks down at his bare shoulder. There is something very wrong. A deep patch of dark blue extends up from his armpit, across the top of the pectoral, over the sharp point of his clavicle. The entire area is oddly misshapen.

Lila feels it gently with her fingertips. Her touch is light but even so, at certain points Niles can barely stand the pressure. "Something's wrong with the joint," Lila says at last. "I don't know for sure. Maybe you're even bleeding inside. You shouldn't put any strain on it at all."

Niles shakes his head. "Fuck that," he says. "Just give me a chance to rest. I'll be okay."

"I don't know," Lila begins.

"Just let me rest," Niles says, "just be quiet and let me rest. All right?"

"Okay," Lila says, standing up, "get some rest."

Niles leans back against the pine log, while Lila takes their dishes down by the stream to wash. He closes his eyes and in the quiet of the clearing lets his mind wander. On the other side of the range, he thinks, they will find a cave—huge slabs of cool granite fallen together, nothing immense, but good shelter, with a small fast trout-filled stream running beside it, and high thick trees for shade and cover. They will build an oven, he thinks, to bake bread, and a pit to smoke fish, and perhaps, down lower, on the brushy banks of the stream, they will find an early-ripening patch of berries, twenty or thirty feet square. And if the fishing is good and the rice and the flour hold out, maybe they can even last three weeks, a month, whittling down their appetites from the bloated standards of civilization to the more precise demands of necessity. They will live simply, saying little, growing peaceful and strong, and Niles' shoulder will heal quickly. They will build careful, smokeless fires at sunset and stare into the coals and forge a new plan, a new idea, as solid as the rock that shelters them, for how they will live when they leave the hills.

"C'mon," Lila is saying, "c'mon, wake up." She is shaking, very gently, his unhurt shoulder. "If we want to get over that pass today," she says, "we've got to get moving."

Niles opens his eyes. Lila's long brown hair is hanging down toward his face as she leans over him. The shadows around him have grown longer since he closed his eyes. "Jesus," he says, "yes. Let's get going."

"How do you feel?" Lila asks.

Niles pushes off from the rotten log with his good arm and rises to his feet. He is slightly dizzy, but he figures it is only because he has so recently awakened. "Fine," he says. "Let's move."

Lila holds out her hand, two aspirin tablets white on her palm. "Take these," she says. "We've got about thirty. They should last a little while."

From here the trail steepens, and the terrain grows rocky and barren, except for occasional clumps of pine and stretches of tight green brush. Niles feels as if he views the trail, the trees, Lila, all through a thin and persistent covering of gauze, and he steps slowly and carefully. The aspirin, he is certain, will soon help.

It is after they have covered two more miles that they first see the helicopter. It grows from a tiny buzzing dot in the unbroken blue of the western sky, running a zig-zag course below them at the boundaries of the wilderness area, and as they watch, it draws nearer and louder, flying very low.

"We better get off the trail," Niles says.

They leave the unsheltered path and retreat into a nearby stand of pines. The helicopter draws closer, until, through the tight branches, they can see that it is painted black and white, with a bulging plexiglass bubble that reflects the afternoon sun like the bulbous eye of an insect. Soon it has approached within a few hundred yards, running a long diagonal course over the trail, and Niles and Lila stay well hidden, silently hugging a tall face of rock overhung by pine branches. When it is closest, almost directly overhead, the road of the 'copter engine drowns out all other sound, and then, in minutes, the noise of the helicopter drifts toward the south, and it begins to grow wavering and faint.

Leaning against the cool surface of the rock, Niles keeps his eyes closed long after the sound has receded. The throb of his shoulder, the dull sleepless ache in his head, the sudden threat of the helicopter, all combine to exhaust him, and he says nothing.

"Ah," Lila says, when the sound of the helicopter is no more and Niles has been silent for a long time, "you think that was for us?"

"I don't know what else they'd be doing."

"But how could they know?" Lila says. "How could they know where to look?"

Niles says nothing, gazing at the stubbly grass around their feet, and Lila does not look directly at him. He knows they are both thinking of Delores. "It doesn't make any difference," Niles says finally. "If they know, they know."

A slight breeze comes up, brushing their faces, moving the pine branches. "What now?" Lila says.

Niles shakes his head.

"If they're coming back," Lila says, "maybe we should stay off the trail."

Niles gazes in the direction the helicopter disappeared. If they are sure enough to use a helicopter, he knows, they will search on the ground as well. "We'll keep going," he says. "That's our only chance. We have to keep going." He turns his back to Lila. "Can you get the map out?"

She unties the top of his pack, trying not to disturb its balance on his shoulders, and hands him the map.

He unfolds it and stares at the light green paper, the flowing brown contour lines. For a moment it makes no sense. He cannot think where they are. It is ridiculous: he is very good with maps.

"We're here," Lila says, pointing.

"I know," Niles says, and then he locates the pass they must cross, and he tries to count the contour lines between. The lines are fine and very close together and it takes him some time. There are ten lines. Ten lines at eighty feet a line is eight hundred feet of elevation. He glances up at the sun. "We've got to get moving," he says.

"Take it easy," Lila says.

"Have you got some more of that aspirin?" Niles asks. "I could use a couple more."

Lila, wordless, gives him more aspirin, and then they leave the trees and move on through the heat and mesquite. Soon they are only a few hundred feet from where the trail suddenly begins to switchback up the rocky face of the pass, almost straight up the steep slope of talus, weaving between the largest boulders as it ascends to the narrow notch between two high peaks. Perhaps half the distance up the switchback there is a final small stand of pine clinging to the rocky slope. Past that it is as barren as the surface of the moon.

"There's not much cover up there," Lila says.

Niles nods but says nothing. His right arm is now so numb that he cannot move his two smallest fingers, and his head stubbornly refuses to clear. "Let's go," he says. "We can rest at those trees."

His booted feet slide like beached boats up the loose granite scree. Lila stays close behind him and he can hear her breathing, hard and steady, and sometimes it mixes with his own and he cannot tell which is which. The afternoon sun throws their shadows, long and gangling, up the slopes beside them, aping their steps. The space between Niles' ears feels empty and hollow, and he no longer thinks of his shoulder at all.

They gain altitude so quickly that Niles can feel the air growing cooler and thinner. The sun remains unclouded. "This trail," Lila says between breaths, "is a bitch."

Niles nods, although the words barely register. When

he looks to his left, he can see, miles distant, to the smog-tinted brown valley still bright with sun, and the steep slopes and convoluted ridges that grow up abruptly from the foothills, and the swelling green stretches of pine and scrub brush that they walked through earlier in the day. There is no sign of the helicopter.

They have come a long way, Niles thinks. They have a long way to go. The pass towers above them. On the other side of the pass, he tells himself, on the other side of the pass they will—

"Hey," Lila says from behind him, "take it easy. Hey!" she says, "watch it!"

Niles has walked into a boulder of granite fully as high as his knee. It hits his shin, as painful as a sharp kick, and he folds, easily, gracefully, turning around until he half-sits, half-stands, stuck in between the boulder and the rocky border of the trail.

"Jesus," Lila says, "are you okay?" She offers him her hand but he continues his half-sit.

Niles stares up at Lila. The sun is directly behind her head and the stray hairs flare out like solar prominences. With all his energy, he concentrates on the moment. "Fine," he says slowly, "I'm fine."

Lila gazes at him for a long time. "I don't think so," she says. "I really don't think so."

After a minute or so they cover the last fifty yards to the stand of pines that dot the trail. Inside the pines there is a small flat space of packed dirt. Lila helps Niles slide his pack off, carefully, gingerly, and she leans it against one of the pines. Niles sits down, hard. Far in the distance below them, the smoggy valley is brown cottony haze.

Lila slips the bedroll from her shoulders, watching the sky carefully, and sets it on the ground. "Put your head here," she says.

Niles does not reply. He is staring at the dirt, hands pressed to the sides of his head. "I am all right," he says at last. "It's the sun," he says softly, "the god-damned sun."

Lila kneels beside him and feels his forehead with the back of her hand. "Let me see your shoulder," she says.

"Don't worry," Niles repeats.

Lila unbuttons his shirt. Niles tries to shrug it off his shoulders but it does not work. Lila pulls the shirt off cautiously.

"It's hot," she says, feeling the blue flesh that has now taken on a faint crimson tinge at the edges of the discoloration. "I don't know," she says, "maybe it's infected. A bone chip, something like that."

"No," Niles shakes his head. "If I rest, I'll be all right."

Lila looks at him for a long time. "Maybe we should go back," she says finally. "I think you're kind of sick."

"No," Niles says, "no, wrong, I'm fine."

"I think we should go back," Lila says. "I think you need some help."

Niles leans his head back against the trunk of a pine, feels a bit of resiny pitch stick into his hair. "I don't need help," he says.

Lila says nothing, and then, far in the distance, they hear the buzzing again. The helicopter is making a return pass, this time closer to the highway, perhaps three miles from the base of the pass. Niles and Lila stay still and watch as the small black dot moves slowly across the pine-covered terrain, flying an angling search pattern. At last it turns, rotating on the axis of its blades, and, accelerating, disappears in the brown haze of the valley.

"We're all right," Niles says softly. "I think they missed us."

Lila says nothing for a moment. "You need a doctor," she tells him finally. "We should go down and try to find a doctor."

"If we go back down they'll put me in jail."

"They'll put you in a hospital first."

Niles shakes his head. Lila opens the canteen and soaks her blue bandanna with cool water.

"You think I can't keep up, right?" Niles says. "You think we'll both get caught because I can't keep up."

Lila starts to tie the bandanna around his forehead. The damp cloth is so cold it feels like a spike into his brain. "I think being dead in the mountains isn't going to do you any good at all," she says quietly. "You know what happens when bone tissue gets infected?"

Niles shakes his head again. "Just five minutes," he says. "Just give me five minutes rest, and I'll be ready." He leans back against the tree, feels the pitch sticky in his hair.

Lila says nothing more. She moves away and sits, her back to Niles, on a small rock that overlooks the valley and the curving trail they have walked.

Niles is starting to feel much stronger. The situation deserves respect, but it is not hopeless. What they are doing is important enough to take chances for.

There is little wind coming up the face of the pass and the stand of pines is still and quiet. Niles closes his eyes and the minutes move by quickly in the silence. Lila continues to stare out over the valley. At last Niles sits upright, shakes his head gently, tries to rub sensation into his lower arm. He feels strong, newly alert, ready to move. "Let's go," he says to Lila. "We can make it to the top in twenty minutes."

Lila is briefly silent. She does not turn around. "No," she says finally. "I'm not going."

conclusion

the santa teresa mountains

At first Niles thinks he has not heard correctly.

"I don't want to go," Lila repeats. "This is as far as I go."

"But," Niles says, "but I'm fine. I'll be all right."

Lila simply shakes her head.

"But the mountains," Niles says. "The mountains are your idea."

"It's not going to work," Lila tells him flatly. "It could have worked, someday it might work, but it won't work now."

"We're almost there," Niles says, sitting up straighter, "we're almost—"

"You're going to kill yourself if you stay out there," Lila says. "If that's what you want to do, you don't need me."

Niles stares down at the packed dirt. The ground is covered with dry pine needles and a few small pine cones. One of the cones has been stripped by a squirrel. "That's it?" he says at last.

Lila nods, finally turns to look at him. "That's it."

"I'm not going back," Niles says. "I can't." He tries to rise to his feet but the dizziness overtakes him and he sits again, quickly, to let his head clear.

"Do you know how sick you are?" Lila asks. "You must know."

Niles opens his mouth, closes it. Something is uncomfortably wrong with his stomach.

"I'm going back down," Lila says. "I'll go alone, and I'll wait for you and hope you come back. But I'm not going with you."

Niles closes his eyes, concentrates for a moment. It is a bluff, he thinks. Lila will change her mind. "All right," he says, "I'll do it myself."

He stands again, and begins to walk over to the pack, stepping carefully, knowing that Lila is watching him closely. He unties the top of the pack and is about to reach inside for the map when they hear the sound. It is at first so distant and faint that it is impossible to identify. It is not the helicopter, but neither is it anything natural. The oddness of the sound freezes them where they stand, barely breathng. Niles watches the cloudless sky. Lila stares out over the trail below them. "Hey," Lila says finally, very quietly, "hey. There's horses down there."

"Horses?"

Lila squints into the distance. "Two of them," she says, "I think."

Niles stays low, pulls himself over next to Lila, follows the direction of her gaze, down onto the thin winding trail far below them. There are more than two. Three or four small dots of brown have emerged from the trees perhaps a mile from the base of the pass. They are moving quickly up the trail, and, as Niles and Lila watch, they understand the sound that first attracted their attention. It is the sound of dogs.

The dogs are still invisible in the distance but their long high baying now drifts up easily to the slope of the pass. "Those are hunting dogs," Lila says. "They've got some kind of hounds."

Niles stares out over the valley a little longer. The horses are moving fast, directly up the trail. At last he turns slowly and sits down against the pine trunk and sighs, long and quietly.

"They're for us," Lila says, "aren't they?"

Niles' head is suddenly very clear. He leans back and feels the anger and exhaustion in his throat, a bitter extract like the taste of electricity. "I don't know what else they'd be doing."

Lila is kneeling at the edge of the trees, still looking out over the terrain below them. "They're riding fast," she says. "What should we do?"

Niles leans back against the pine and closes his eyes and he says nothing for a long time. At last he looks at Lila. "It doesn't change your plans."

Lila stares at him. "We can't just sit here," she says.

Niles shakes his head. "Nothing to do," he says. "There's nothing to do." Either direction they move, they will be immediately visible on the barren trail. Although the horses will have to go slow on the rough climb up the pass, Niles will go even slower.

Lila looks out over the valley, looks back at Niles. "Do something," she says. "We've got to do *something*. Dammit," she says, "you can't just . . ." Her sentence trails off, she turns back, and the sound of the dogs drifts up, like distant distorted music.

"Fuck 'em," Niles says quietly, unmoving, "fuck 'em."

"I could start down by myself," Lila says. "I could go down and tell them I'm alone, that we split up."

"Won't do any good," Niles says. He moves back over next to Lila. From their vantage point halfway up the pass they can see miles to the west; the distant valley, the slopes now increasingly shadowed as the sun sinks toward the cloudless brown horizon.

"There has to be something," Lila says, her voice strained, "there's got to be something we can do."

"Sure," Niles says, so quietly that Lila almost cannot hear. He turns away, goes back to his pine trees, and as he sits he realizes that he is ready to give up. That if they will give him a soft bed and a good doctor and a big meal in the morning, he will not be sad to see it over. It is pointless, a waste of time and energy, to go through the last moves of the game, a useless effort to escape an air tight checkmate. Even here, nine thousand feet above the factory and the jail, there is no way to escape. For two years, since the day he walked out of the Labs, he has been working out the steps of an elaborate and inevitable dance. And this is the last little movement—the end of the fantasy.

He looks up and sees that Lila is at the pack, digging frantically through its contents. "What are you doing?" he asks.

Lila does not look up. She continues to paw through the pack until at last she pulls out the mindfogger, the small metal case grey and dull in the shade of the clearing. "Here," she says, holding the box out to Niles. "Here. We can use this."

Niles stares at the mindfogger. The dented corner reflects the angled light of the sun as Lila moves her hands.

"Come on," she says. "It's all we've got."

Niles looks at Lila for a long time. "No," he says.

"No?" Lila says, her expression frozen. "They'll be here in five minutes. What do you mean, no?"

"I mean no," Niles says. "There's no point to it. That's just dragging it out. It's giving it to them." With his good hand he feels around his feet and picks up a fist-sized chunk of granite. "Bring it here," Niles says. "I don't want them to have it."

Lila looks at the rock in his hand. "You're going to wreck it?" she says. "You're going to give up without even trying?"

"Bring it here," Niles repeats.

"No." Lila takes a step back and holds the mindfogger even more tightly. "It's your last chance," she says. "It's all you've got, it's"—she punches the red microswitch with her finger—"it's the only way you'll"—and then her voice trails off and she looks closely at the box in her hand. She pushes the switch again, and then there is a space of silence, punctuated only by the distant staccato yelping of the dogs.

"It's broken," Lila says at last, slowly. "It doesn't work anymore."

"Broken?" Niles says.

Lila pushes the switch again. "See?" she says. "It doesn't do anything."

"Push it harder," Niles says.

Lila pushes it harder and still nothing. She looks at Niles.

"Goddamnit," Niles says, "let me see it." He walks over and takes the small box and shakes it gently. An intermittent circuit, even one he is about to destroy, is something he will never be able to ignore. He holds the box, and with the thumb of his good hand he punches the switch, very hard.

"Ah," Lila says, "ah."

The warm cerebral humming spreads through their minds like a heavy syrup. Lila's tense face relaxes, she smiles, and then Niles pushes the switch again.

"The switch is bad," he says.

"Come on," Lila says. "We've got to try."

Niles sets the box down on the hard packed dirt. He grips the rock in his left hand and raises it above his head, but just as he is about to smash the aluminum case, he notices something odd. A few drops of clear liquid have begun to exude from the seams of the chassis box. He takes out his pocket knife and removes the screws from the case and pulls the two halves of the box apart and stares into the interior of the circuitry and sees something he does not understand at all.

The clear plastic case of one of the nickel-cadmium batteries has cracked and leaked acid into the chassis, and now the tiny components and circuits mounted on the partially decayed phenolic board are a bright garden of chemical corrosion. The plastic insulation of some of the wiring harnesses has been burned and melted by the powerful acid, and the copper conductors are shorted together. Niles holds out the two halves of the box and Lila peers inside.

"It's ruined," Niles says slowly, looking up at Lila. "It's completely ruined. It can't possibly work."

"But you just made it work." Lila stares at Niles, and for a moment there is silence. The wind rises up the face of the pass, carrying the sound of the dogs, now louder and more distinct. "It's in you now," she says finally. "You do it yourself. The box is just decoration."

"No," Niles says, "the box does it. I designed it. I designed it to." Yet the circuitry is useless. The battery, he realizes, must have expanded and cracked in the lower pressure of the mountain altitude.

"Do it," Lila says. "Make it happen again."

Niles turns the disabled chassis over in his hands until the switch faces him. He presses it, and the mindfog spreads, and then he presses it again and it is gone. For a moment he closes his eyes. He is delirious, he thinks, he is confused, the fever has reached his head. His mind refuses the implication of his act, and his thinking rushes to assemble an explanation from pieces that will never again fit together the old way.

Lila reaches out and takes the mindfogger from Niles' hands and she drops it onto the rough ground. "Do it again," she says, watching him closely. "Do it once more."

Niles looks at the assemblage of metal and plastic and semiconductor spilled on the dirt at his feet. He imagines that once more he is pressing the small red switch. This time he presses it only inside his own head. The mindfog, as thick and warm and pervasive as ever, fills the pine clearing, and after a moment Niles makes it disappear.

When it is gone, Lila stares at him. "You do it yourself," she says. "You don't need the box anymore."

"But the box," Niles insists, still unwilling to believe, not trusting his senses, "the box—"

"Maybe it taught you," Lila says slowly, touching the ruined device with the toe of her boot, "maybe it was a charm. But it's in your head now. Nobody can take it away from you."

Niles shakes his head and turns from Lila and stares out over the foothills toward the brown valley. "Impossible," he says. "It's impossible."

Lila looks at him. "I don't think it's impossible at all."

Niles glances over the edge of the clearing. The horses and riders, moving fast, have started up the pass. The clatter of hooves on loose granite is like a slow, endless rockfall. Niles turns back to Lila. "Break up the mindfogger," he tells her. "It's useless now anyway."

Niles watches the slow progress of the search party, the dogs ranging a few yards before the horses, as the sounds of pounding granite, cracking plastic, issue from behind him. For a moment he concentrates on the image of the tiny red switch, and when he turns around, he sees Lila on her knees over the mindfogger, shaded by the pines, a chunk of granite in one half-raised hand, but the hand has slowed and she is smiling and gazing around with a pleasant expression. Niles realizes that this time he feels nothing himself, and he turns back and pushes the switch again. The pounding resumes.

"It's done." Lila says after a moment. She slides the mashed mindfogger, now a mass of dented aluminum and splintered plastic, in near the top of the pack. She looks at Niles across the small space of the clearing. "What now?"

Quite suddenly, like a movie image abruptly focused, it makes sense to Niles. What has happened has nothing to do with fevered thinking or delirium. It is as natural as the erosion of granite, the growth of the pines, the flowering of the manzanita; the fruition of a process begun a thousand centuries before; a first step, out of the ocean and onto the land. The sense of it, the rightness, the inevitability, form up inside him like a solid core of tempered steel. He has no idea where it will go from here; it can only grow to fit. But of one thing Niles is certain—this is only a beginning.

His right arm is numb, and at the shoulder still painful, but it no longer matters so much. He stands beside the pack, kneels, balances it on one knee, and swings it up onto his back. Lila watches him with puzzled concern, her question still hanging in the air. Standing, a bit uncertainly, he puts his good arm around her for a moment, balancing himself, and he squeezes the back of her neck. "I'm going," he says.

She stares at him, frowns, looks down at the horses, back at him. In the yellowing rays of the sun Lila's skin is dark, her eyes very blue, very serious.

Niles shoulders his pack higher.

Lila picks up the bedroll in one quick movement and slides the thick rope loops over her shoulders and begins to walk, with long strides, toward the steep trail to the top of the pass.

"Hold it," Niles says quietly after her. "Wrong way."

Lila stops, looks back at Niles, frowning.

"This way," Niles says, nodding back down the trail. He leans to one side, balances the pack on his shoulders, tightening the waist belt. "The way we came. We'll go down and meet them."

Lila stares at him for a moment, and then she begins to smile.

They start back down the trail, retracing their steps, walking into the soft orange of the smog-tinged sunset over the valley, walking now quite slowly, Niles with his hands in his pockets, stepping out carefully, taking time to admire the shadowed country far below them, Lila brushing her hair back, securing the top button of her shirt against the chill.

Soon they are less than fifty yards from the band of horsemen, who have stopped to block the trail, unmoving, casting long thin shadows up the rocky slope. There are four mounted county sheriffs, khaki-clad, with hounds and rifles and a saddle-bag radio. All four rifles are held steadily on Niles and Lila.

"Real slowly," the big deputy in front calls, holding his rifle with one hand, pushing his mirrored sunglasses up with the other. "Real slowly and with your hands raised."

Niles stops walking and Lila catches up with him and they stand for a moment, unmoving.

"Listen," Niles says to her quietly, as the dusk wind blows up from the valley, past the deputies, and wraps them in a new chill cold. "Listen: if I can learn, you can learn. As soon as I can, I'll teach you."

"That's a promise?"

Niles nods. "That's my promise."

Below them on the trail, the lead deputy reins his horse a few feet forward and aims his rifle more precisely. He leans back easily in his saddle. "Hands over your heads," he says, more loudly. "Right now."

Niles looks back down the trail at the horsemen and, without moving, he smiles. The rifle barrels hold steady briefly, then waver, then sink slowly in gentle arcs, almost with the grace of softening wax, and then one, and two, and now four deputies begin to grin back.

"Why don't we borrow a couple of their horses," Niles says to Lila, and he touches her arm and they begin to walk down the trail and then nothing is ever exactly the same again.

BESTSELLERS FROM DELL

fiction

☐ GHOSTBOAT
  by George Simpson and Neal Burger...... $1.95 (5421-00)
☐ EAGLE IN THE SKY by Wilbur Smith....... $1.95 (4592-06)
☐ MARATHON MAN by William Goldman..... $1.95 (5502-02)
☐ THREE DAYS OF THE CONDOR
  by James Grady..................... $1.50 (7570-13)
☐ THE RHINEMANN EXCHANGE
  by Robert Ludlum................... $1.95 (5079-13)
☐ THE OTHER SIDE OF MIDNIGHT
  by Sidney Sheldon.................. $1.75 (6067-07)
☐ CROSS-COUNTRY by Herbert Kastle........ $1.95 (4585-05)
☐ BIG NICKEL by Calder Willingham......... $1.95 (5390-07)
☐ DARK VICTORY by Charles Israel.......... $1.50 (1655-06)

non-fiction

☐ HOLLYWOOD BABYLON by Kenneth Anger.. $5.95 (5325-07)
☐ THE LAST TESTAMENT OF LUCKY LUCIANO
  by Martin A. Gosch and Richard Hammer... $1.95 (4940-21)
☐ THE ULTRA SECRET by F.W. Winterbotham... $1.95 (9061-07)
☐ MEETING AT POTSDAM by Charles L. Mee, Jr. $1.95 (5449-08)
☐ MORRIS by Mary Daniels................. $1.50 (5673-05)
☐ ERIC by Doris Lund................... $1.75 (4586-04)
☐ INSTANT FITNESS FOR TOTAL HEALTH
  by Stanley Reichman, M.D............... $1.50 (4070-07)
☐ DON'T SAY YES WHEN YOU WANT TO
  SAY NO by Herbert Fensterheim, Ph.D. and
  Jean Baer........................... $1.95 (5413-00)
☐ MILTON BERLE: An Autobiography......... $1.95 (5626-11)

Buy them at your local bookstore or send this page to the address below:

DELL BOOKS
P.O. BOX 1000, PINEBROOK, N.J. 07058

Please send me the books I have checked above. I am enclosing $_____
(please add 35¢ per copy to cover postage and handling). Send check or
money order—no cash or C.O.D.'s.

Mr/Mrs/Miss _____

Address _____

City _____ State/Zip _____

Offer expires 4/77